DIRTY DOZEN

A J.J. Graves Mystery

LILIANA HART

ALSO BY LILIANA HART

JJ Graves Mystery Series

Dirty Little Secrets

A Dirty Shame

Dirty Rotten Scoundrel

Down and Dirty

Dirty Deeds

Dirty Laundry

Dirty Money

A Dirty Job

Dirty Devil

Playing Dirty

Dirty Martini

Dirty Dozen

Dirty Minds

Dirty Weekend

Dirty Looks

Dirty Liars

Dirty Valentine

Addison Holmes Mystery Series

Whiskey Rebellion

Whiskey Sour

Whiskey For Breakfast

Whiskey, You're The Devil

Whiskey on the Rocks

Whiskey Tango Foxtrot

Whiskey and Gunpowder

Whiskey Lullaby

The Scarlet Chronicles

Bouncing Betty

Hand Grenade Helen

Front Line Francis

The Harley and Davidson Mystery Series

The Farmer's Slaughter

A Tisket a Casket

I Saw Mommy Killing Santa Claus

Get Your Murder Running

Deceased and Desist

Malice in Wonderland

Tequila Mockingbird

Gone With the Sin

Grime and Punishment

Blazing Rattles

A Salt and Battery

Curl Up and Dye

First Comes Death Then Comes Marriage

To Scott—How did I get so lucky? You support my dreams and keep me stocked with Milk Duds. You love Jesus, me, and our children sacrificially, and anyone who knows you sees how special you are. Our future is bright and blessed. Love you, XOXO

ACKNOWLEDGMENTS

Getting a book to publication takes an amazing team of people. I'm fortunate to have had these people in my corner for years.

To my editors—Imogen Howson and Ava Hodge for always making me better.

To my cover designer—Dar Albert for always blowing me away with your talent.

To my children—You're all so special. You have gifts and abilities beyond measure, and I'm excited to see what God has in store for each of you.

To Scott—thank you for answering a ridiculous amount of law enforcement questions and acting out weird scenarios with me. Any mistakes are mine alone.

To my readers—We made it to book 12 in the series! Thank you for continuing the journey with me and allowing me to do what I love. I have the BEST readers in the world!

Because I could not stop for death,
	He kindly stopped for me;
	The carriage held but just ourselves and
immortality.

— EMILY DICKINSON

I am prepared to meet my Maker.

Whether my Maker is prepared for the great ordeal of meeting me is another matter.

— WINSTON CHURCHILL

The killer watched intently from the balcony as the curtain fell and the crowd erupted into applause. It had been a mediocre performance at best, but for local theater he supposed it could have been much worse.

The Curtain Call was doing a five-day production of the great Oscar Wilde play *Lady Windemere's Fan*. He could only assume that Mr. Wilde would have taken his leave at intermission to go enjoy a nice port and cigar instead of suffering through the occasional botched line and flat attempts at humor.

But Juliet had been perfect. *Juliet*—even her name was perfect. Like a tragic heroine in a long-ago play, she played the role of Lady Windemere brilliantly.

The velvet curtains opened again and the cast came to the stage to take their final bows. He stood with the rest of the crowd, his white gloved hand grasped tightly around the gold lion's head on the end of his walking stick. He put on his top hat and adjusted the burgundy satin scarf around his neck, and then he pulled the watch from the small pocket in his vest to check the time. Timing was everything.

He was dressed like the others in the room, though there had been a few who'd ruined the scene by not dressing in appropriate attire. The Victorian festival in Newcastle was always a community favorite. People came from all over Virginia to attend, and they dressed in period pieces of the times. Restaurants changed their menus and there were concerts and events each night.

He'd been waiting for this week for months. This was the beginning of it all. Tonight the first domino would fall, and there was nothing anyone could do to stop them. His planning and execution would be flawless. Perfection was everything.

The excitement rose up in him so swiftly he had to catch his balance so he didn't fall back into his seat. He locked his knees and stared at Juliet, willing her to look in his direction. He wondered if she saw his face, if she'd know he would be her end.

He was enraptured by her beauty—the translucent quality to her skin, the lush blond curls, and the wide eyes that shone emotion all the way to the back row of the theater. There was an innocence there, even though he knew it was all an illusion. She was anything but innocent.

Just like Lady Windemere, Juliet had become dissatisfied with her husband and searched for a lover elsewhere. She was a whore. And those who sold their bodies had to be punished.

He excused himself past the patrons sitting to his left and exited the row, making his way swiftly down the stairs and out the side door before things became too crowded and he couldn't get into position. He'd watched and searched and planned for months, until the scene played out in his head like a movie.

He checked the watch in his pocket again. The delivery would be arriving soon. He hastened his steps, using his cane to move quickly past the people headed in the opposite direction. They were moving like a school of fish toward the park to watch the fireworks. No one would know what was happening behind the theater. No one would hear her screams. And if everything went as scheduled, no one would find her body until morning. By that time, he'd be preparing for the next one.

The night air slapped cold against his face, but he hardly felt it as he took his position behind the dumpsters in the alley. He removed the knife from inside his jacket, mesmerized as the steel glinted beneath the single streetlight at the corner of the building.

The first firework exploded and the sky lit with red and blue. The people in the park cheered. But he only had eyes for the back door of the theater. He was all alone.

He'd pushed one of the dumpsters closer to the door the night before so he could be within striking distance, and he was glad he'd made the adjustment. Nervous excitement coursed through his veins, and he cursed himself for not doing a run-through in another place—to have the experience of feeling flesh give beneath the knife and the hot rush of blood over his hands. What he'd done to Mother hadn't counted. He'd debated with himself over and over again. Practice made perfect. Mother always told him that.

But in the end he'd decided he didn't need a dress rehearsal. There was something special about Juliet being his first. It was intimate. He'd always remember her because of that. His breath came in shallow pants and he couldn't tell if the moisture on his face was from sweat or tears.

The theater door opened with a slam against the brick and Juliet came into view. There hadn't been time to remove the lacy white confection she wore—the corset and bustle and petticoats—and her stage makeup was harsh under the yellow glow of the streetlight.

She cradled the pink roses he'd sent in her arms, and the note he'd written was clutched in her hand.

"Peter!" she called out. "Where are you? I'm so glad you came! I thought you wouldn't be able to make it."

The joy in her voice at the anticipation of seeing her lover sent a shiver down his spine. That joy was all the reminder he needed to move into action.

The blade slashed quickly across her throat, the blood hot and wet as it hit his cheek. He was disappointed that she hadn't had time to scream. He would've liked to have heard it. But by then it was too late. The anger inside of him boiled and the knife became an instrument of rage.

CHAPTER ONE

Even in my half-conscious state, I felt the mattress dip beside me and I cracked my eyes open.

I noticed two things—it was still dark outside and Jack was holding a cup of coffee under my nose. That could only mean one thing.

My name is J.J. Graves and I'm the coroner for King George County, Virginia. I'm also the owner of the local funeral home, but that job rarely requires me to get out of bed before dawn. The hours before dawn were reserved for dock workers, nursing mothers, and killers. Since I didn't know any dock workers or nursing mothers, I had to assume it was the third option that was about to ruin my day off.

"What time is it?" I asked, scooting to a sitting position against the headboard and taking the mug. Jack had given me the mug for my birthday, and it said, *Coffee, Because Murder is Against the Law.*

"Just after four," Jack said.

He was already dressed in his uniform of jeans and a long-sleeve button-down khaki shirt that had *King George County Sheriff's Office* embroidered over the left breast pocket. He smelled of soap, and I liked that he hadn't shaved, so there was a bit of dark stubble on his face. His eyes were dark—almost black—and alert, which was one of the many things we didn't have in common. Jack was a fantastic morning person, if there was such a thing.

It took me a little longer to acclimate to a new day. My five senses woke slowly—the scent of coffee and Jack's soap—the feel of the sheets soft and warm pulled up to my chest—the sight of the rain that fell like mist through the trees outside our picture window—and the sound of the shower running on full blast in the bathroom. All that was left was the taste of heaven in the cup Jack had put in my hands. He always took good care of me.

I sometimes wondered if I'd ever get tired of the everyday details of marriage, but in my heart I couldn't imagine waking up next to this man every day for the rest of my life and not appreciating the gift that he was.

"Earth to Jaye," he said, his mouth quirked in a half smile.

"Sorry," I said, blinking and taking another sip. The heat burned my tongue, but it was more important that the cobwebs cleared from my mind rather than be concerned about being able to taste anything the rest of the day.

I brought my hand up and touched his cheek, and then I rubbed my thumb across the scar that slashed his eyebrow—a scar I had put there when we were kids.

"You're so handsome," I said, and then I grinned at the uncomfortable look he gave me. "So what happened? Who died?"

His mouth quirked again, and I had a feeling I'd already missed the explanation, but he didn't hold it over my head.

"A call came into dispatch about half an hour ago," Jack said. "A body found in Newcastle."

"Ahh, Victorian week," I said. "Bar fight? Active shooter?"

"Nope," Jack said. "Single victim found in an alley behind the theater by a drunk guy who picked a bad place to use the bathroom."

"Risky for the killer," I said. "And the public urinater Newcastle is crowded this time of year. The theater is a heavily trafficked area."

"Maybe not so risky," he said. "The bars close late, but the drinking is heavy. People stumbling around with metal tankards of ale all dressed up in stupid costumes and making poor life decisions. They usually eventually end up in the park or back at their hotels." He gave a lopsided smile and said, "Or other creative places."

"Ahh," I said. "Those were the good old days. But that still doesn't explain why I'm drinking coffee strong enough to bring back the dead or why you're stalling so my brain actually starts to function."

"Oh, good," Jack said, slapping me lightly on the leg. "You're awake enough if you're thinking that logically. Get out of bed. Shower is already running. Plank and Chen were first on scene and Plank said it was pretty grisly. They've secured the crime scene, but it's an alley, and apparently our costumed witness lost a good bit of his alcohol after seeing the body."

"Lovely," I said, taking Jack's hand so he could help me to my feet, and then I shuffled into the bathroom. "God, I love this job. The glamour and glitz is sometimes overwhelming. Not everyone gets to start their week with death and vomit."

"Ooh, sarcasm." Jack looked into my almost-empty cup and said, "Was there something in there besides coffee?"

"I'm just extra sassy today," I said. "It's like a bonus." And then I stripped and stepped into the shower. "Give me five minutes."

"See you downstairs," Jack said. "I'll put cream in your next cup. I'm not sure I'm up for a day of you being extra sassy."

• • •

I was out of the shower in five minutes, and it took me another five to pull on jeans and an old King George University sweatshirt that had a small mustard stain on the band from a wayward hot dog. I pulled a dark green watch cap over my head and laced up my heavy winter boots.

My favorite thing about watching crime shows on television was how put together everyone looked at a crime scene. The women wore heels and nice suits, nails were manicured, and no hair was out of place. I'd caught sight of myself a couple of times on the news, and I'd had an internal conversation about being a public figure and looking more presentable for public perception. Jack always looked camera ready, but that was genetics more than the time he actually spent on his appearance.

But for my part, it was a short-lived war. Crime scenes were never camera ready or picture perfect. They could be messy. And sometimes the weather added to the mess—rain, snow, cold, extreme heat —it all played a part. When you'd had the experience of walking onto a crime scene with an umbrella to keep brain matter from dripping on your head from a murder/suicide, then you stopped caring about outward appearances and moved toward the practical. And I was very practical.

It was February, and Virginia in February tended to be wet most days—either from rain or snow or a combination thereof—and it was cold. As soon as Jack mentioned that a body had been found in an alley my mind went to all the probabilities of what kind of shape the victim would be in.

Not to mention all the generally disgusting things that could be found in an alley that might contaminate my scene. Rats wreaked havoc on dead bodies.

I bounded down the stairs and Jack was waiting for me by the front door with my heavy waterproof jacket and a to-go cup of coffee. I grabbed my medical bag off the entry table, made sure my camera was inside, and then Jack took it from me and hefted it over his shoulder.

"Wait a second," I said. "What about Doug?"

"I left him a note on the refrigerator," Jack said. "That way I know he'll get it."

It had been five days since Doug Carver had moved in with us. To say that it had been an adjustment was an understatement, but we still felt like it was the right decision to make. Doug was the nephew of Jack's best friend, Ben, and Doug wasn't a typical teenager. He was off-the-charts smart, to the point that he'd been under house arrest for a good part of his teenage years for hacking into high-security government institutions.

Carver had been the one to turn Doug in, and oddly enough, Doug didn't hold it against him. They were peas in a pod, and Carver had told Doug in no uncertain terms that their gifts were to be used for good and not for evil.

Doug had agreed, but he'd still had to wear an ankle bracelet and do his schoolwork online. He was sixteen and finishing up a couple of college degrees, and his mom had done everything she could for him. He needed something to keep him busy and out of trouble, and Jack and I could provide that for him by letting him help with the occasional case.

So he'd packed his bags and we'd redecorated a suite on the second floor that he could call his own. Jack came from money, and he'd never been shy about spending it, but if we ever went broke I was pretty sure it would be because Doug ate us out of our budget.

"Good thinking," I said. "You don't think we should wake him up for class or anything?"

"Class is his responsibility," Jack said. "He'll be fine."

Jack locked the front door behind us, and then we walked under the covered porch to the portico where his Tahoe and my Suburban were parked.

"How long has it been raining?" I asked.

A drizzle fell in the darkness, but it was the kind of rain that soaked everything and everyone through to the skin and seeped into the bones along with the cold. I'd take the fat drops from a thunderstorm any day of the week over this crap.

"I checked the weather reports and it looks like the rain started just after two. And it's not supposed to let up anytime soon."

I went to open the door of the Suburban and realized it was already running and the heat was on full blast. Jack had come out and started things up while I'd been getting ready. I grabbed the lapels of his jacket and pulled him in for a kiss. Jack was great about the little things, and I hoped I never took them for granted.

"Thank you," I said, taking my bag from him and tossing it onto the passenger seat. "You're the best."

"You can pay me back later," he said, giving me a grin that had my blood heating beneath my skin. "I'll follow you to the scene."

———

Newcastle was a half-hour drive from our house, and it was still dark by the time we pulled up to the scene.

Newcastle was one of the four towns that made up King George County—along with Bloody Mary, King George Proper, and Nottingham—and just like all the towns in King George, it had its own vibe and quirks. Newcastle had an artistic, bohemian feel that the rest of the county didn't have. There were as many yoga studios as coffee shops, and the demographics leaned toward up-and-coming late-twenty to early thirty-somethings who still hadn't figured out if they wanted a career or to lose themselves in their creativity and starve for a living.

The buildings downtown were historic, and even the new apartments they'd recently built around the park had an old-world feel to them. The streets were cobbled and gas streetlamps and iron benches were placed strategically along the sidewalks.

But during the Victorian festival, they took things to another level. The city council did their best to make sure everything was authentic as it could be, even going so far as to not allow vehicles in the cordoned-off streets. Only foot traffic or horse and buggy were allowed. Jack and I drove around the barricades and made our way down the cobbled streets until the Curtain Call came into view.

It was the corner building facing the park, and it looked like a white birthday cake with all the ornamental carvings and arches and columns a baroque architect could possibly add. There was a second-floor balcony that looked out over the park and the streets, and the theater would host a cocktail hour for donors before each show. Anyone who was anyone wanted to be seen on that balcony. When I was a kid there'd been a fistfight between two of the wealthier men in town, and one of them had fallen over the rail and cracked his head on the sidewalk. People still talked about it as if it had happened recently.

There were a couple of black-and-whites with lights flashing parked near the entrance of the alley, and there were two ambulances several yards away near the park entrance. I pulled in beside Jack and turned off the car, and then grabbed my bag and hopped out. The stocking cap I wore would be soaked through before long, so I pulled the hood of my jacket up for the time being. The cold was bitter, and I felt the warmth from Jack's good deeds of the morning start to fade away.

Jack left his lights flashing and then met me at the back of the Suburban to help pull out the gurney. There had been many days after I'd inherited the funeral home where I'd had no choice but to work solo—I hadn't been able to afford any help —especially after the financial and legal mess my parents had left me in after they'd faked their deaths.

But business at the funeral home had picked up and I'd been able to hire Emmy Lu and Sheldon to keep things running on a day-to-day basis. My parental problems had mostly resolved themselves over the last several months. I tried not to think about it.

Things on the coroner side of my career were going well too. The county council had voted to include a stipend for the coroner's office in the new bond that had recently been passed, so I felt justified in hiring Lily on part-time while she was going through her doctoral work to be a pathologist.

I wasn't quite comfortable with the newfound peace in my life. It was a new experience, and I knew a good part of it was because of Jack. He'd always been the best part of my life. But still, there were times when I waited for the other shoe to fall.

But despite my good fortune in the employee department, four thirty was way too early to call in for Sheldon or Lily for help. Nobody got paid enough for that. This was a job that fell squarely to me as the appointed coroner for the county. Besides, it was Monday, and the office was closed on Mondays because our weekends were typically full with funerals and viewings. I would've felt like a crumb calling anyone in on their day off.

The only good thing about responding to a call at this time of the morning was that the crowd was light and the media was slow to action. Living in a county the size of King George had its benefits— the population wasn't huge and people tended to do exactly what they wanted in the time they wanted to do it in. Of course, that was also one of the cons of living in a county the size of King George. Everyone was as stubborn as a mule, and things got done when they got done. And no sooner.

Officer Plank stood at the corner of the theater, his Day-Glo rain jacket dripping water. He looked miserable, but he rushed over to take the other end of the gurney from me.

"Hey, sheriff," Plank said. "Doc." He nodded. "Been waiting on you guys. Scene is all secured, but this rain is a killer."

Plank hadn't been out of the academy for long, but he'd had some of the shine rubbed off of him during the last couple of cases we'd worked. He was a lot more confident in his abilities, but there was still an innocence in him that had him seeking Jack's approval and encouragement on a job well done.

"Good work," Jack said, surveying the cordoned-off area.

Plank was young, early twenties, and his face was soft and round with a single dimple in his cheek that appeared when he smiled. His cheeks were red with the cold and he was in his full winter uniform. He wore a black wool cap over his ears, and white puffs of air escaped from his mouth when he spoke.

"Where's Chen?" Jack asked.

"I told her I'd wait out here for you guys," he said. "She was shivering so bad she could barely talk, so Detective Cole took her with him inside the theater to look around. She didn't look happy about it. You know how tough she is, but she wasn't going to argue with an order from Cole."

"I was wondering who drew this one," Jack said. "How long has Cole been here?"

"About half an hour," Plank said. "He called in for a couple of uniforms to come help. Somebody has to dig through the dumpsters."

Jack grimaced in sympathy. "What about the guy who found her? Has Cole talked to him yet?"

"Just the basics," Plank said. "Cole thought you might want to sit in on that one. Guy's a real weirdo. Totally caught up in the whole Victorian thing. Insisted Cole call him Lord Buckley."

Plank pointed to the two ambulances parked at an angle next to the park entrance. A group of young people sat on the back of the ambulances, legs swinging and talking to each other animatedly.

But it was the man sucking in oxygen in the center of the group who caught my attention. They were all dressed in high-quality costumes, but there was something haughty and regal about the man that set him apart from the others.

"The kid with the oxygen is the one who found the body," Plank said. "ID says his name is Thomas Chapman, a.k.a. Lord Buckley."

His comment about the kid made me smile because Plank was probably a few years younger than Chapman.

"He said he went into the alley to take a leak," Plank continued, and then he looked at me with abject horror that he might have offended my delicate ears. A flush of red crept up his neck and cheeks.

Plank was one of those guys who had been raised by a good Southern mom who'd taught good Southern etiquette. I figured cop life would break him of all those habits in the first couple of months, but Mrs. Plank's teaching obviously left a lasting impression. I'd suggested to Jack that she come teach a few classes at the academy.

"I can guarantee that people have done much worse things than taking a leak in that alley," I said.

"Right," Plank said. "Well, umm, the pubs have been open until three all week because of the festival. And Lord Buckley told Cole he and his friends had last call at the Rose and Arms. That's about all he was able to get out before he started puking again. Threw up so much the EMTs gave him something to calm him down."

"Some people don't handle murders well," I said. "Go figure."

"He messed up your crime scene," Plank said. "He sicked up most of what he drank. And then got rid of the rest of it once Cole started talking to him. I think Cole made him nervous. He's probably stone-cold sober now though."

"Great," I said, squenching my nose in disgust. "Can't wait to wade through that."

The gurney bumped over the cobbled road until we got to the entrance of the alley, where the cobblestone transitioned to asphalt so the garbage trucks could access the dumpster area more easily.

The drizzle was steady and cold and I wished I could keep on the fur-lined leather gloves I wore, but I'd ruined more than one nice pair of gloves trying to stay warm while I looked over a body. In the end, it wasn't worth the trouble.

Urine and vomit and garbage combined to assault my senses, but I recognized the fresh, coppery scent of blood over the putridness of it all.

"The scene is clear and ready for me?" I asked Plank.

"Yes, ma'am," he said. "Detective Cole said it's all yours."

I stopped the gurney and placed my bag on top, taking a quick glance at all of the yellow numbered evidence markers. The rain hadn't washed away all of the blood, which meant there had been a lot of it.

I could partially see the victim from behind one of the dumpsters—a pale arm surrounded by something fluffy and white.

"That's a lot of blood spatter," Jack said, echoing my thoughts. He took out his flashlight and shone it over the markered areas.

I removed my leather gloves and grabbed surgical gloves from the pack I kept in my bag, slipping them on expertly. Then I handed a pair to Jack. I liked to take my own pictures at each scene, so I put my digital Nikon around my neck for easier access.

"I'll grab your bag," Jack said, lifting it from the gurney. "It'll be a mess otherwise."

"Thanks," I said. "Let's take a look at her."

"If you don't mind, sheriff," Plank said, his face going pale, "I think I'll keep my post out front and make sure no one gets through. I got enough of a look at her before."

"Sure, Plank," Jack said, slapping him on the shoulder and following behind me.

"The innocence doesn't last long," I whispered as we moved toward the dumpsters.

"I know," Jack said. "I feel guilty when I see guys like Plank enter the academy. He really wants to serve. He wants to help the public. And then we put him through hell and don't bother to mention that he'll suffer from a lifetime of PTSD or that he'll struggle with relationships because of the things he's seen."

"Your psychology degree is showing," I said.

"I like to dust it off every now and then so it doesn't feel like a complete waste of time or money."

"I definitely think you got your money's worth," I said, coming to a stop as we rounded the dumpster and got our first clear look at the victim. "Maybe you could do a quick profile of our killer since you're dusting it off."

"Wow," Jack said. "Sick. Definitely sick."

CHAPTER TWO

"Is that your professional opinion?" I asked, carefully maneuvering my way around the victim's intestines that had spilled out across the pavement.

"I could go with whack-job or psychopath too," he said. "I don't like to paint myself into a corner."

"Plank was right," I said. "This crime scene is a mess." The area reeked of alcohol and vomit where Thomas Chapman had lost his buzz. "It looks like he tripped over her. And there's been some rodent activity. It doesn't take long in an environment like this."

Jack inched his way behind me so his back was to the brick wall, and he held my bag down so I could dig inside and grab a thermometer.

"She's still warm," I said, after taking her temperature. "There's barely any rigor in her fingers. The guy that found her didn't miss her killer by much."

A crime scene like this one could be over-whelming. There were a lot of variables at play.

"She wasn't killed here," Jack said, shining his flashlight toward the back door of the theater and the yellow markers that indicated the smear of blood across the pavement.

"She was dragged," I said, taking several pictures of the victim. I was careful to touch her as little as possible. "With all that blood pooled by the door he would have sliced her throat there. I can see the arterial spray on the walls. So much rage."

I gently touched the gaping wounds at her neck with my gloved finger. "Left to right strike," I said, pointing to the area where the knife first entered the body. "Would've sliced right into the carotid artery and then he jerked it down. It's a deep wound, and it's a smooth cut. There's only a small amount of tissue connecting the head to the body."

"Big knife," Jack said. "That first slice would have covered him in blood. There would've been no way to avoid it."

"No," I agreed. "And then he stabbed her in the throat again just for good measure. She's got multiple stab wounds in the chest and abdomen." Her dress was in tatters. "Then he gutted her."

"You think he did that postmortem?" Jack asked.

"I think he did it after he dragged her back here behind the dumpster," I said. "There's some rodent activity along the soft tissue, and these dumpsters are probably full of rats. When Chapman found her and tripped over her he probably helped the disembowelment process."

"Hope that guy has a good therapist," Jack said.

I grunted and picked up her hand, checking to see if there was anything visible under the nails or defensive wounds on her wrists or arms. "She didn't even have time to defend." I bagged both of her hands, and then went about the painstaking task of bagging her intestines.

"No visible signs of sexual assault," I said, checking her legs and to see if she still wore undergarments. "She doesn't appear to be missing any clothing. I'm assuming Cole didn't find any ID on the victim?"

"You'd assume right," Cole said. "This one's a doozy, huh? Not at all how I wanted to be woken up in the middle of the night."

Cole reminded me of a modern-day cowboy with his Wrangler jeans and boots. It was rare to see him without a cowboy hat, but tonight he had on his Gore-Tex jacket and a neoprene skullcap pulled low over his dark blond hair. He had a slow drawl and Southern manners that many thought made him slow in the head, but he had a brilliant detective mind and a quick wit.

Cole was a good cop, and he'd worked with Jack for a long time. I liked him and trusted him in a professional capacity. The jury was still out on the personal front. Cole had a reputation among the ladies as being irresistible for the first couple of months. Then he'd lose interest and move on to the next. He was nice about it, and he'd somehow managed to untangle himself without scores of women wanting to punch him in the face.

I'd never cared about Cole's love life before, but it was different now because he was dating my pathology assistant, Lily. They'd only been dating a few weeks and there was a significant difference in their ages. The way Lily looked at him made me nervous, and we were all watching the pair of them like animals at the zoo to see if they were going to mate or end up killing each other.

"You and me both," I said. "There's not much more I can do here with the delicate state of her organs. I want to get her bagged and back to the lab as soon as possible."

"I brought Lily with me," Cole said. He grinned sheepishly and shrugged. "She was there when I got the call, and she figured you'd need help with transport."

"Good," I said, for once grateful that he and Lily were shacking up. "It saves time. Did you get an identification on the victim?"

"Sure did," Cole said. "Juliet Dunnegan. I found her purse in one of the dressing rooms backstage. Driver's license picture matches the victim. I ran a quick check on her. No outstanding warrants. She's married. Address is a few miles from here."

"Have you checked with dispatch to see if the husband called in to report when she didn't come home for the night?" Jack asked.

"No calls came in," Cole said. "He might have

gone to bed knowing she'd be in late. It's early yet. He might still be asleep."

"Maybe so," Jack said. "What do you want to do?"

Cole sighed. "What I want to do is go home and get back into bed. But I guess what we need to do is clear the scene so we can start digging through these dumpsters to see if the killer dumped the murder weapon. No point trying to pull prints from anything with it being so wet."

I stood when I saw Lily heading in our direction, pushing the gurney we'd left back in the middle of the alley. Lily was literally one of the most beautiful women I'd ever seen, and she was also the kindest and most humble. She somehow managed to make the sweats and over-sized coat that clearly belonged to Cole look good.

"You ready to bag her?" Lily asked.

"Yeah," I said. "I've got all the pictures I can get. I don't want to roll her because of obvious reasons. I'm worried about the head staying intact during transport, and I don't want to lose any more of her tissue than we already have."

Lily and I worked to get Juliet Dunnegan bagged, and it turned out to be a wet and messy process. The rain was relentless. The pavement and the victim were both slippery when wet, and my foot slipped while trying to maneuver Juliet into the bag.

"Careful," Jack said, catching me before I ended

up with my backside in things I didn't want to think about.

I was out of breath from the exertion, and I mumbled, "Thanks," as I got my footing back under me.

By the time Juliet was loaded into the back of the Suburban, none of us were in a good mood and I was desperately wishing for another cup of coffee.

"My bones hurt they're so cold," I said, peeling off my gloves and tossing them in a trash bag. I pulled my fur-lined gloves out of my bag and put them back on, but it didn't do much good at this point.

"I'll take the body back to the lab," Lily said. "I know you like to stay on scene during the initial investigation."

"How will you get her unloaded?" I asked.

"I'll call Sheldon," she said. "It's not like he's been out all night partying. I'll bet you fifty bucks he's been listening to the police scanner his mom got him for Christmas and he's sitting by the phone waiting for your call. Bless his heart. I hate to disappoint him."

Sheldon was a good assistant, but his social gift was with the dead instead of the living. He was sweet in a golden retriever kind of way, but he took a lot of time and energy. If anyone but Lily had said what she had, I would've thought they were being sarcastic, but she treated Sheldon like a kid brother and she had more patience than Job.

"That's a sucker's bet," I said, handing her the

keys to the Suburban. "I'll catch a ride back with Jack."

People with better manners probably would have turned away to give Lily and Cole a few minutes of privacy to say their goodbyes, but Jack and I weren't those people. We watched openly as Cole whispered something in Lily's ear that made her blush, and then they kissed goodbye.

Lily drove off and then Cole turned and arched a brow at us. "Any comments from the peanut gallery?"

"Kiss looked like it needs some work," Jack said.

I snorted out a laugh and said, "Maybe monogamy is making him lose his technique."

Cole blew out a breath. "Y'all can shut up now. Don't we have a crime scene to investigate?"

"That kiss looked like a crime scene to me," Jack murmured, making me burst out into laughter. "I'm kidding!" Jack held his hands up in surrender, but his grin was unrepentant.

"Laugh all you want," Cole said, slapping Jack on the shoulder. "But I'm serious about her. I've never been this serious about anyone before."

"Wow," I said. "You only turned a little green when you said that. It must be love."

"I didn't say love," he hurried to say. "I said I was serious about her. I just don't know what that looks like yet."

"Other than the fact that I've known you for twenty years and you've always been dead scared of commitment," Jack said. "Why the protest about love? Are you anti-love?"

We retraced our steps to the alley and then made our way inside the theater where it was dry and warm.

"I'm not anti-love," he said, squirming uncomfortably. "I'm just not exactly sure what it feels like. I've never been in love before. How do I know if it's love or lust? What if it's all just physical?"

"You'll know," Jack and I both said at the same time.

"The fact that you're so scared of it you're white in the face should tell you you're on the right track," Jack said. "You've been in lust lots of times. If this feels different it's because it is. Lust will fade. What you have to figure out is what your foundation is made of? Friendship? Companionship? Respect?"

"Your psychology is showing," Cole said.

"What are you scared of?" Jack asked, ignoring the comment.

Cole was quiet for a bit, and I wondered if he was going to answer. "She wants me to meet her parents."

I would've laughed if it weren't for the sickening look of dread on his face.

"I've met her parents," I said. "They're nice people. They're not a firing squad."

"That's because you're not sleeping with their daughter," Cold said. "How would you feel if your daughter brought home a man seventeen years older than she was, and that man was me?"

Jack and I had only recently been talking about children, and the thought of having a daughter one day still made my heart skip a beat in complete panic. And then the thought of that daughter bringing home someone like Cole brought on an entirely new feeling altogether.

"Exactly," Cold said after a prolonged silence.

Jack looked at me with wild-eyed panic, and I knew he'd had the same thought as I had. Cole would be lucky if Lily's dad didn't murder him before appetizers were served.

"Look," Jack said. "At the end of the day all any parent wants to know is that their child is loved and well taken care of. When you can give Lily those things, then you'll be ready to meet her parents. Good talk. But now that my fingers and toes aren't numb anymore, let's get back to the case."

The transition between topics wasn't as smooth as Jack normally managed, but I had to give him props considering the land mine our previous conversation had dodged.

"Dressing room is through here," Cole said, obviously glad for the reprieve in conversation.

I'd never been backstage at the Curtain Call before. The front part of the theater was for show—ornate carvings and murals on the ceilings reminiscent of famed Italian artists. The walls and curtains were a deep burgundy velvet and there were gold accents throughout. No expense had been spared in restoring the two-hundred-year-old historic theater.

But backstage was a different story. The walls were white plaster, the halls were narrow, and the dressing rooms were cramped. It looked like a bomb had gone off with papers and costumes and flowers everywhere. There were empty champagne bottles and glasses, and if I had to guess, it looked like the cast and crew had decided to celebrate closing night by going out to party and worry about cleaning up later.

"We're going to have to talk to all of the cast and crew once daylight hits," Cole said. "See if we can establish a timeline. She's got the biggest dressing room, not that that's saying much."

The room was too cramped for all of us to fit inside, so I stood in the doorway and watched Jack and Cole. They were both big men, and standing shoulder to shoulder they took up almost the entire width of the room. A rack crammed with costumes was shoved against one wall, and a vanity with bright lights held more makeup than a department-store counter. Every other available space was filled with vases of flowers.

"There were flower petals outside by the door," Jack said. "Crime scene tagged them."

"Good eye," Cole said. "I bagged a bouquet and a note attached before you arrived. One of those big expensive bouquets. Don't ask me how I know that. The note was from someone named Peter. The card was a soggy mess, so no chance of prints. But the florist shop logo was on there, so we'll run it down and see who placed the order."

"Peter?" I asked. "The husband?"

Cole smiled. "Nope. Husband is Brian Dunnegan. But obviously whoever Peter is he's someone important enough that she'd run out back to meet him."

"We'll need to establish a timeline and see when the performance ended," Jack said.

"She was still dressed in costume," I said. "She comes backstage after it's over. There's a ton of flowers in here, but she runs outside with the ones from Peter in her arms."

"Someone handed them directly to her," Cole said. "We'll run down the delivery service along with the flower shop. Obviously Peter is someone important to her. Important enough that when he says he's waiting for her in the alley she stops every-thing she's doing and goes to him. Our killer is waiting for her right outside the door, and she doesn't get far before he delivers the killing blow. At that point the killer is covered in blood and then pulls her body behind the dumpsters."

Jack nodded thoughtfully. "Wanted to hide her long enough so she wasn't found right away."

"Let's go meet Lord Buckley," Cole said. "Maybe he's sober enough to fill in some of the blanks."

We walked back out into the alley and Plank and Chen were standing in front of the dumpsters holding a couple of evidence bags and staring at the officers who had drawn the dumpster short straw.

"Any luck?" Cole asked.

Chen held up a bag with a wicked-looking knife inside. "Dumpster kept it from getting wet. Maybe you'll be able to grab some prints from it along with a blood match to the victim."

"Nice find," Jack said, approvingly.

"That's not all," Plank said, holding up another bag. "Got a bloody scarf and coat."

"We'll take it with us once you're through," Jack said. "Did you get any statements?"

"From everyone but Lord Buckley," Chen said, rolling her eyes. "He kept insisting we call him that. But none of the others saw anything other than Buckley running out of the alley screaming his head off. But we got all their statements and sent them home. Buckley is still in the back of the ambulance waiting for you."

"Thanks," Cole said. "Hopefully he has more to say than gagging sounds now. I'm a sympathetic puker."

"I remember," Jack said, grimacing.

"What bothers you about the murder weapon and clothes?" I asked once we were out of the alley. "I thought you'd be happier about finding that much evidence this soon."

"It worries me that we found that much evidence this soon and that close to the body," Jack said. "Which leads me to believe that we'll find only what the killer wants us to find. I don't like it when killers try to play with us."

The EMTs were huddled together a few feet from Thomas Chapman. The oxygen had been removed and he had a warming blanket around his shoulders. I hadn't met him yet, but he was one of those people I disliked on sight.

"You've kept me waiting far too long," Chapman said in a British accent. "I've been through enough tonight and I need to go home and rest. I'm going to be filing a complaint first thing."

"Make sure you address it to Sheriff Lawson," Jack said.

"It looks like the EMTs have been taking good care of you," Cole said reasonably. "When I first introduced myself you weren't in any shape to answer questions. You're looking a lot better now."

Thomas Chapman was somewhere in his late twenties. He was tall and thin, his face angular and his cheekbones high and reminiscent of some long-ago aristocracy. His hair was dark and slightly wavy and his mustache was neatly trimmed.

He wore formal black beneath the warming blanket and a slightly crushed top hat sat beside him on the back of the ambulance.

"I want to go home," Chapman said again. "I have early engagements and need my rest."

"Mr. Chapman," Cole said. "The sooner you answer our questions the sooner you can go home. A woman is dead. Maybe you can refocus on her instead of yourself."

He paled at the mention of the woman and licked his lips. "I...I don't wish to talk about her. It was a terrible misunderstanding. There's nothing I can tell you. And I prefer you call me Lord Buckley."

"Mr. Chapman," Cole said, ignoring the request. "What time did you and your friends come downtown tonight?"

At first I thought he might not answer. I wasn't sure what Chapman was playing at, insisting that we call him Lord Buckley. He could be crazy or delusional. Or he might be one of those nerds who was seriously into role-play.

Chapman blew out a breath and I winced at the smell, and fought the urge to take a step back. He reeked of alcohol and other things.

"We all met up for dinner around seven," he said. "My friends and I, we go big for the Victorian festival every year. We totally immerse ourselves in the week. My great-great-grandfather was Lord Buckley, so I use his name." He shrugged, looking less haughty and more pathetic.

"Where'd you eat dinner?" Cole asked impatiently. "Walk us through your night up until you found our victim."

"We ate the four-course dinner at the Ivy," he said, losing the British accent. "We made reservations months ago. Then we caught the nine o'clock showing of *Lady Windemere's Fan* at the Curtain Call, but we left at intermission because it was a snooze fest. We headed over to the Knight's Tale after that for drinks."

"You told one of the other officers you were drinking at the Rose and Arms," Cole said.

"Yeah, but that was later," Chapman said. "We were at the Knight's Tale until midnight when the fireworks started. Then we headed over to the park with everyone else. When the fireworks were done we ended up at the Rose and Arms. I don't remember a whole lot after that. We drank a lot."

"Do you remember going into the alley?" Cole asked.

Chapman was looking a little green around the gills again and the three of us instinctively took a small step back just in case.

He nodded and let the blanket fall from around his shoulders to his waist. "We were just being stupid. You know how it is. We were all drunk and everything was funny. I was planning to go back to Jenny's place with her and hook up for the night. We do that from time to time. When we left the Rose and Arms we just kind of walked around singing and stuff, but everything had shut down and the rain was getting worse.

"I had to take a leak so I ran into the alley," he said. "My friend Brent took a leak in the street, but I wasn't that brave so I headed into the alley." His voice got very quiet. "I should've just stayed in the street. I didn't see her at first. I was just minding my business and peeing against the wall, but I saw the blood. It was everywhere, and then I followed the trail. That's when I saw her."

He closed his eyes, and I knew he was reliving it in his head. Things like that weren't easy to erase from memory.

"I don't really remember a lot after that," he said. "I might have yelled. I...I tripped over her. The ground was slippery with her blood. And then I fell down and I got sick." He held up his hands and I could see where they were scraped raw from the fall.

"Did you know her?" Cole asked.

"I recognized her," Chapman said. "She was the woman from the play. But I don't know her. Her throat." He swallowed several times trying to get his composure. "It was gaping wide open. There was nothing there."

"Did you notice anyone else hanging out around the alley?" Cole asked.

Chapman half smiled and said, "I don't think I would've noticed if there were a hundred people outside the alley. The only things on my mind were taking a leak and getting Jenny in bed, in that order. Everything else is kind of fuzzy."

"We'll be in touch if we need to ask more questions," Cole said. "We'll have an officer drop you home."

"I think I'll have them drop me at Jenny's," he said. "I don't really feel like being alone with my thoughts."

By the time we walked back to Jack's Tahoe, Chen and Plank were coming out of the alley with evidence bags.

"I think we've found everything we're going to for now," Chen said. "We'll have the crime scene team do another sweep in full daylight. For now we've closed the tops of the dumpsters to keep as much rain out as we can, and we'll block access to the alley. We'll keep watch until the techs can get here in a couple hours."

Jack took the evidence bags and nodded. "Send the rookies to grab you some coffee and y'all warm up in the car while you're waiting. It should be pretty quiet for a while."

"I'm not going to argue with that," Plank said. "But I'll let Chen give the orders for coffee. I graduated the academy with those guys."

Jack put the evidence bags in his Tahoe and then turned to Cole. "What are you thinking?"

"I'm thinking it's early as hell, and everyone is still in bed. Including the husband of our victim."

"What do you say we wake him up and see how surprised he is about his wife's death?"

"I was thinking the same thing," Cole said.

"Weird," I said. "Because I was thinking how I wished the rookies were bringing us coffee too."

"The donut place is about to open," Jack said. "We'll drive through. I could use a pick-me-up too."

"Donuts always give me a pick-me-up," Cole said, heading to his truck. "Meet you there."

CHAPTER THREE

THE DONUT SHOP HAD JUST OPENED AS WE PULLED into the drive-thru, and by the time we reached Brian Dunnegan's house fifteen minutes later I was warm, fed, and caffeinated.

"You've got powdered sugar on the front of your jacket," Jack said as we parked in front of a contemporary townhome in a new subdivision. It was white with black trim and lots of windows and it sat about six inches from neighbors on either side.

"Very Stepford," I said, brushing at the powdered sugar.

Jack grunted. "Claustrophobic."

There were no lights on inside the house. The only lights on the whole street were the identical gas lanterns that hung from every porch and Cole's headlights as he pulled up behind us. We were thrown into darkness again when he turned them off.

Cole got out of the truck and rocked back on

the heels of his boots, surveying the area. "Creepy," he said. "People have no imagination."

"Maybe it's a cult street," I said. "Have y'all ever been called to a scene out here?"

"Not that I know of," Jack said. "I'm not familiar with this neighborhood."

"I bet a neighborhood like this buries all their problems in the backyard," I said, conspiratorially.

"This is a zombie neighborhood," Cole said. "Freaks me out. If hands start popping out of the ground and grabbing at my ankles I'm leaving y'all here."

"Good to know where your protect and serve limits are," Jack said.

Our footsteps were mostly silent over the wet pavement as we made our way to the small porch. It wouldn't be long before a neighborhood like this started stirring to get ready for the workweek—unless they were just going to bed after a long night of feeding.

Jack pressed the doorbell and we waited. Then he pressed it again.

"Can I help you?" an irritated and distorted voice said through the speaker in the doorbell.

"Brian Dunnegan?" Jack said. "I'm Sheriff Lawson. We need to talk with you."

There was more than a minute of silence before a light came on in the entryway and the locks clicked open. The door cracked open a couple of inches.

"Do you know what time it is?" Brian asked. "I'd like to see some identification."

Jack held up his badge for inspection and the man nodded. "Sheriff Lawson," Jack repeated. "This is Detective Cole and Dr. Graves."

Dunnegan's annoyance didn't dissipate, but he opened the door all the way. "I recognize you now. I've seen your picture in the news. You might as well come in, but I'm going to have to start getting ready for work before too long."

"We won't take much of your time," Jack assured him.

Dunnegan knew. The nerves were obvious as he looked at each of us in turn, and he didn't know what to do with his hands so he shoved them in the pockets of his robe. We walked into a foyer as sterile and cold as the outside of the house.

Brian Dunnegan was in his early fifties, but he could've passed for a decade younger. He was fit, and it was obvious he spent a good amount of time in the gym. His face was unlined and his brown hair was silver at the temples cut severely short. He didn't seem like the kind of man who spent a lot of time smiling. He wore black-framed glasses and a gray robe over gray pajamas.

"Why don't we sit down?" Jack suggested.

"I really don't have a lot of time," Brian said. "Is this about the fundraising for the sheriff's office? We have a PR person at my firm who handles all of that, and I'm going to file a formal complaint about the hours you choose to harass the populace."

"We're here on official business, Mr. Dunnegan," Jack said. "You might want to sit down."

"What's wrong?" Brian asked, his face going pale. "Is it my daughter? Is she okay?" His hands came out of his robe pockets and they were balled into fists. "Did someone hurt her?

People handled fear and grief in different ways, and we'd seen just about everything, but Brian Dunnegan didn't even have information yet and he was already in a fighting posture. That said a lot about a man.

I did a quick scan of what we could see of the house. It didn't look like the kind of house where children lived. Everything was very white and very sterile. There were no family pictures on the walls or clutter on the counters or a purse or jacket hanging over a chair—just very tasteful paintings and sculptures. It looked like a model home, as if no one actually lived there.

"Your daughter is fine," Jack said.

"Then I don't understand," Dunnegan said.

"We're here about your wife," Jack continued. "I'm sorry to say her body was found early this morning."

Quick was the best way. Deep down people always knew their loved ones were gone when we showed up at the door. It was kinder not to make them wonder. But Brian Dunnegan's behavior was odd. He'd not mentioned his wife once, and he wasn't wearing a wedding ring. I looked at Jack in confusion. Maybe we had the wrong Brian Dunnegan.

"My wife?" he asked.

"We have this address listed as the home of Juliet Dunnegan," Jack said. "Is that correct?"

"Juliet?" Brian asked as if he just now recalled he had a wife. "That's impossible. I'm sure she's in her bedroom."

I raised my brows at that. No wonder he hadn't reported her missing. Brian left us and went down the hallway, his robe flapping behind him, and he pushed open the door to a room at the end of the hall.

"Juliet," we heard him call. "Juliet! Where are you? Stop causing drama." We heard a door slam and he called her again.

He appeared in the hallway moments later, a thread of anger overriding the surprise that he hadn't found her lurking in a closet. "She's not there. Her bed hasn't been slept in. This is so like her."

"Let's sit down, Mr. Dunnegan," Jack said again. "We need to ask you a few questions."

This time Jack didn't give him an option, but he moved into the living room and stood in front of a white leather chair positioned near the fireplace.

"Dr. Graves is the coroner for the county."

"You saw her?" Brian asked me. "You're sure it's Juliet? She's really good with makeup and costumes."

"The victim we identified this morning was not

faking," I said, a little sharper than I'd usually speak when dealing with someone who'd just lost a loved one. But Brian Dunnegan was rubbing me the wrong way. "We were able to compare the victim with the driver's license photo from her purse."

I moved over to the stiff white leather couch and took a seat. It was impossibly uncomfortable, and I had the fleeting thought that if the Dunnegans ever had company over they probably didn't stay for long.

Brian moved stiffly to the matching couch across from me and sat down, and then Cole took the spot next to him so he was flanked. There was something unusual in Dunnegan's expression, and I wasn't sure if it was guilt or fear, but it certainly wasn't grief.

"When was the last time you saw your wife?" Jack asked.

"I don't understand any of this," Brian said. "I'd like to see the body. I just don't believe it's her. Juliet loves being the center of attention. It's her theater background. She can't help herself."

"Believe me, Mr. Dunnegan," Jack said dryly. "There are better ways to prank someone than to have your throat slit."

Two hot spots of color appeared on Dunnegan's cheeks and he stared angrily at Jack. "It's not unreasonable to want proof," he said haughtily. "Especially considering her background. She's always done whatever she could to get my attention. And since I told her I wanted a divorce I was expecting her to pull something drastic like this."

"When did you tell her you wanted a divorce?" Jack asked.

Dunnegan pressed his lips together. "Do I need an attorney?"

"That's up to you," Jack said. "But you mentioned before you didn't have much time for us, so I'm assuming you don't want to spend the better part of your day down at the station."

"I sent her a text on Saturday," he said.

"You told your wife you want a divorce in a text message?" Jack asked.

"Come on, now, sheriff," Cole said, his drawl more pronounced than usual. "You know how it is in situations like this. Tempers flare and emotions are high. Sometimes a text message is the best way to go."

Dunnegan looked at Cole as if he was the only one of us who had any sense. Cole liked playing good cop. He said he liked to sucker the suspect in and then watch them trip over their own feet once they realized they'd gone too far. Of course, I hadn't expected to go from giving death news to suspect in such a short time span. But I guessed while we were here it was better to kill two birds with one stone, especially since Dunnegan seemed like the type of man who'd have really irritating attorneys.

"She's never here," Dunnegan said. "She's been at that stupid festival all week, coming in at all hours of the night. When she bothers to come home at all. Juliet is a spoiled party girl who has no idea what she wants in life unless it's spending other people's money. We weren't married long before I realized it was best to go about my own life and build my company. Marriage is expensive. Divorce is more expensive." He shrugged as if that should explain it all.

"It looks like you've been very successful," Cole said. "What kind of company do you have?"

"I'm an architect," he said. "I have a firm out of DC, but I recently moved my main offices to King George. I was able to get a great spot overlooking the Potomac and I designed our new building. It's a great advertisement for potential clients because they want to come see it firsthand. It's been featured in several architectural journals."

"You were never worried when Juliet didn't come home?" Jack asked.

"Not at all," Dunnegan said. "Sometimes she'd text if she remembered. More often than not, she didn't. She's hated this house since I built it, and according to her I'm cold and emotionally distant. She's found plenty of warmth in other places during the twelve years we've been married."

"The two of you have children?" Cole asked. "You mentioned your daughter?"

"No," Dunnegan said. "Juliet and I never had children, thank God. She's too much of a child herself. I have a daughter from a previous marriage."

"You mentioned Juliet liked to be the center of

attention," Jack said. "Has anyone ever given her unwanted attention before?"

Dunnegan snorted. "Believe me. There was no such thing as unwanted attention to Juliet. If a man meets her criteria—meaning he's attractive, has money, and gives her lots of stuff—then she'll play whatever role she has to until she gets bored."

"You've not noticed anyone unusual in the neighborhood over the last couple of weeks?" Cole asked. "This seems like the type of place where neighbors notice things."

"Oh, they do," Dunnegan said. "Which is why everyone in the neighborhood knows exactly the kind of woman Juliet is." And then he paused and corrected himself. "Was. But despite Juliet's multitude of faults, she was very popular and well liked. When can I move forward with funeral plans? I'd like to get the details taken care of as soon as possible. I need to call my attorneys and my secretary so she'll know I'm going to be late today. I've got important meetings this afternoon."

"I'll do the autopsy this morning," I said. "If nothing significant comes up in my findings I should be able to release her tomorrow."

Dunnegan got to his feet and said, "If you'll excuse me, I really do have a lot to do today. I'm already behind schedule."

Jack stood and pulled a business card from the inside pocket of his coat. "You can get in touch with me or Detective Cole if you think of anything that might help us find your wife's killer. He's still out there somewhere. You wouldn't want this to happen to anyone else."

Dunnegan nodded stiffly and showed us out. The lock clicked behind us.

"I don't think we'll be talking to Mr. Dunnegan again without his attorney," Cole said.

"I think you're probably right," Jack said. "I'm interested to see what Dunnegan would've lost in a divorce settlement and what he'll gain through the death of his wife."

"On it," Cole said.

The rain was still coming down in a steady drizzle, but it had gotten colder and I wished I'd worn my longer jacket. I think it was vanity that kept it hidden in the back of my closet. My great-grandmother had worn a down puffy coat for the short amount of time I'd known her because she was always cold and that's the only thing that kept her warm. There was something inside me that rebelled about looking like my great-grandmother, even if my jeans were damp and the cold was seeping into my bones.

"What about a phone?" I asked. "He said he texted her about the divorce on Saturday."

"We found one in her dressing room, but it wasn't charged," Cole said. "It's with evidence. I can have someone plug it in and we'll take a look. How many people can I pull in on this?"

"Martinez just cleared a case," Jack said. "Use him. And Plank and Chen might as well help with the interviews and any paperwork since they're already up to speed. If you need anyone else let me know. I'm sure Plank would love some time with Wachowski."

Cole laughed. "I heard they were going to shack up. Does Plank's mama know about that?"

"Wachowski isn't one to hide her light under a bushel," Jack said.

"They all grow up so fast," I said. "Come on. There are things frozen on me that do not need frostbite if I hope to have children one day."

"Hey, you hardly looked like you wanted to vomit at all at the mention of children," Cole said, grinning as he got into his truck. "Must be getting used to the idea."

"Shut up," I said, but I could see him laughing as he drove away.

Jack turned the heater up on full blast, and it didn't take long to warm up since it hadn't taken long to deliver the news of Juliet Dunnegan's murder.

"Can you drop me at the funeral home?" I asked. "I'll go ahead and get started on Juliet. Should only take me a couple of hours."

"Sure," Jack said. "I need to check in at the office and see what else is going on. There was a shooting a couple of hours ago in King George. Armed robbery at a convenience store. Clerk took one in the arm tackling the guy to the ground, but it looks like he's going to be okay."

"Lucky guy," I said. "That could've ended badly."

"Clerk said this was the third robbery this month and he's sick of those punk bastards thinking he's an easy mark," Jack said. "His words, not mine. He told Nash he would have shot the guy in the face with the sawed-off he brought to work, but he didn't have time to reach for it."

"Well, in that case, I'm glad he jumped him," I said. "I've waded through enough blood and guts today and getting shot with a sawed-off never ends well."

Jack drove around the square that connected the four towns of King George County. It was where all the municipal buildings and the courthouse were located, but the county had done a revitalization several years ago that had brought unique shops and events to the Towne Square.

Jack's wipers swished back and forth like a metronome, and I looked out the side window at the soggy cupids and hearts that decorated the lampposts. It was another week until Valentine's Day, and with it would come the Love Run 5K that would end at the courthouse and a matchmaking event for singles at the Knights of Columbus Hall.

He turned left off the square and drove another block and the funeral home came into view. It sat large and stately on the corner of Catherine of Aragon and Anne Boleyn. It was a traditional, red-bricked Colonial my grandparents had built decades ago, and like most things involving my family, I had a love-hate relationship with it. My grandmother had met her death after she'd fallen out of the third-story window. Legend was that my grandfather had helped her with a strong push, but it had never been proven. Graves men were good at evading the law.

I'm fourth-generation mortician. It was my great-grandparents who'd opened Graves Funeral Home back in the early part of the twentieth century. They'd started as gravediggers and earned enough money to open the first funeral home in Bloody Mary. I wasn't naïve. My ancestry wasn't known for being law-abiding citizens. So more than likely they earned enough money to open the first funeral home from grave robbing instead of grave digging.

"You're worried about something," I said, just as Jack was pulling into the driveway of the funeral home. Even the towering oaks in the front yard looked like they were tired of the wet and cold. I felt their pain.

"Carver," Jack said immediately.

I hmmed in agreement. Doug wasn't the only Carver who'd moved to Bloody Mary in the last week.

"Something is going on there," I said. "He's trying not to show it, but he's scared."

"I know," Jack said. "Michelle is a partner in a very prestigious law firm, they've got the four girls so they're close to Michelle's mother, and Carver is close to work and all of his doctors for rehab. It doesn't make any sense at all to move away like they're doing."

"Michelle said she's decided to resign from the firm and put out a shingle for herself here," I said. "I don't think she knows what's going on either. She didn't seem to know why it was the best thing for their family, only that Ben thought it was. She's not going to let him keep it from her for long though. You know how she is. She'll let him tug the line for a good distance and then she'll reel him in and whack him over the head."

Jack laughed. "Nice analogy. And exactly how you have to deal with Carver."

"I hope he's not in trouble," I said. "They've been through enough over the last year."

Carver had been one of many who'd been collateral damage at the hands of my father. Carver had been helping us on a case and was carrying sensitive information when my dad ran him off the road and down into a ravine at high speed. Carver's SUV had smashed headlong into a tree, crushing his pelvis and breaking multiple bones in his body, not to mention the internal injuries. It was a miracle he was still alive at all, and Carver had been through hell these last months trying to relearn everything he'd lost. But his mind was still as sharp as ever, and there was a part of him that knew the chances that he'd be confined to the wheelchair he was currently in might last forever.

"I think it's probably safe to say that whatever is going on, he's worried for his safety and the safety of Michelle and the girls. I'm not going to let him swim out much further either before I reel him in and conk him on the head. I'd like to know if we're about to get a federal level spike in crime in my county. And I want to make sure they have the kind of protection that computers and alarm systems can't offer."

Carver was in charge of all cybersecurity and the technology side of things for the FBI. I wasn't exactly sure what his official title was, but his direct boss was the FBI director and he always joked that his security clearance was higher than the president's. I didn't doubt it. Carver had considerable resources in the personal computers he'd built, and I was pretty sure he could run every country in the world from his wheelchair at the touch of a button.

But his personal computers were on the unorthodox side, especially since they all sounded like they were high-class call girls and he talked to them on a level that was much too intimate for someone who didn't exist. After meeting Carver's computer women, I wasn't exactly excited about artificial intelligence gaining in popularity.

"Thanks for the ride," I said, leaning over to kiss Jack goodbye.

"Text me when you're done and we'll grab some lunch if you've got time," he said.

I brightened up at that. "I'll make time for lunch. I had a dream about chips and queso last night. You know what that means."

"Maybe you're pregnant?" Jack quipped.

"I was going to say it means it's time for a visit to

Taco Joe's." My mind was drawing a blank. "What? What did you say?"

"I think you blacked out for a moment," Jack said, unbuckling my seat belt for me. "Sorry, I can't help myself. Your reaction is just too funny. I know you're not ready yet. I won't pressure you. But I'm going to have fun with it from time to time. I'll just keep talking about it real subtle like until you're used to the idea."

"I hate to break it to you, but I think you need to look up the definition of subtle in the dictionary." I shook my head, grabbed the evidence bags, and I half fell out of the Tahoe.

"You're buying lunch," I said, and closed the door, hurrying up the ramp that led to the side door of the funeral home.

I had to give Jack credit. His subtlety was weighing on me like a ton of bricks.

CHAPTER FOUR

The fresh smell of coffee assaulted my nose when I entered the funeral home. I hung my jacket and winter gear in the mudroom, and took off my all-weather boots in exchange for the Crocs I kept under the bench.

The funeral home was divided into public and private spaces, and the kitchen and everything to the right of it was considered private, including my office and the lab in the basement.

Lily and Sheldon were sitting at the island with a box of donuts between them, drinking coffee, when I walked in. Their heads were pressed together conspiratorially, and I wondered what gossip they were sharing. If there were two more opposite people on the planet it had to be Lily and Sheldon, but they'd somehow formed a friendship that ran true and deep.

"What's going on?" I asked, eyeing them suspiciously.

"I was just telling Sheldon there's a girl I want to introduce him to," Lily said. "She's the manager at the shipping store. I think they'd be a good match. She said she doesn't have a boyfriend and she has her own apartment." Lily waggled her eyebrows at Sheldon and he turned scarlet. "You should come with me one morning and I'll introduce you."

"I don't have anything to ship," Sheldon said.

I closed my eyes and shook my head.

"I always have things to ship," Lily said. "I get all these subscription boxes and then I end up having to return half the stuff in them."

"Then why do you sign up for the subscription boxes?" I asked.

"Because I always have hope that what's in them will be as cute as what they advertise," she said. "And if we don't have hope, we don't have anything."

"I don't know if that's true," Sheldon said. "There's no data on that to my knowledge."

"You'll have to take my word for it," Lily said.

"Okay," Sheldon said.

Lily beamed and took another donut. "It's settled then. We'll go tomorrow during our lunch break."

Sheldon looked like he'd been hit in the face with a two-by-four, so I moved to the coffeepot in hopes it would help untangle the conversation I'd just been witness to. I stared at it for a few seconds, trying to remember how many cups I'd already had, and I figured if I couldn't remember then I should probably opt for a bottle of water from the fridge.

"Thanks for coming in on your day off," I told them, opening the water and taking a drink.

"Oh, sure," Lily said. "My plans for the day got cancelled anyway and I'm mostly caught up on schoolwork. That was a lie. I'm never going to be caught up on schoolwork. But any time you're working and learning it should technically count as schoolwork, right?"

"That's the philosophy I used in med school," I told her.

"Besides, my mind can't focus on any of that stuff. Cole and I had all these plans. Do you know this is the first time we've both had a day off at the same time? Whenever we make plans he gets called into work. Or if he has a day off he gets called into work. How are we supposed to spend any time together?"

"That's cop life," I said. "But working together makes it easier. I wish I could tell you it'll get better, but it doesn't. I've found that if you don't make plans at all you don't get disappointed. Then when he actually does have time off you do something spontaneous and then it's more of a surprise."

"That makes no sense," Sheldon said.

"That's cop life too," I said, smiling.

"Did you know the divorce rate among sworn officers is between 60 and 70 percent?" Sheldon asked. "And statistically speaking, when one of the couple is in a non-first responder position, the divorce rate is even higher. I'm not sure you've really thought your relationship with Detective Cole through."

Lily didn't seem offended at all. "I appreciate your concern, Sheldon. We're just taking things one step at a time. I know what the statistics say, but we can't live our lives based on someone else's data."

"Did you know divorce rates in the mortuary industry are very low?" he asked, his eyes wide behind his Coke bottle glasses. "I think it's because we have a greater understanding of the finality of life, and continuing to look for spouses because of dissatisfaction is a waste of time and energy, and it shortens the lifespan."

"Oh, Sheldon," Lily said, patting his hand gently. "You're such a romantic. You'll find a lucky lady someday who looks forward to hearing about all that knowledge in your head. Maybe as soon as tomorrow."

"I hope she can cook tuna casserole," he said. "We should ask her. It's my favorite, and women really don't put a lot of emphasis on learning to cook these days."

"Want a donut?" Lily asked me, laughter in her eyes.

"I've already had one," I said, even as I was reaching for a plain glazed. "Did you get our guest settled?"

"We tagged her and started the paperwork for

you," Lily said. "She's in the cooler. I thought you'd be a lot longer."

"Yeah, well, the victim's husband isn't exactly the grieving widower," I said. "Since y'all are here, you can come down and assist if you want or you can head home. Up to you."

Lily shrugged. "I'm good to stay and help. Cole texted and said he's up to his neck in canvassing the area and looking for witnesses."

"I can stay too," Sheldon said. "Mother has her blackjack Bible study group on Mondays."

My mouth quirked but I managed to stifle the laughter so I didn't hurt his feelings. "I've never thought to put the Bible and blackjack together before."

"Mother says if they can cast lots in the Bible than she can sure as heck cast them in her living room with mimosas."

"Never thought of it that way," I said, finishing off my donut before heading over to the locked door that led down to the lab.

I typed in the code and the seal around the door released with a *whoosh*. It was a thick metal insulated door that had been installed by my parents to protect the sanctity of their criminal mortuary business.

I had to hand it to my parents. They'd set the bar high for criminals everywhere. At least until my mom decided she was better off working for the CIA so she didn't end up behind bars. I'm still not sure she's not a criminal, and since we haven't gotten together for a mother-daughter bonding moment since she shot my dad in our living room, I'm fine with wondering.

The air was cold when we stepped onto the landing that led down to the lab, and the lights came on automatically. My parents had made sure everything was state of the art. My lab, in the middle of small-town Bloody Mary, was better equipped than almost every state lab on the east coast. Though it's not like my parents were having to wait for state funding to receive and deliver contraband through the bodies that came through here.

We opted to take the lift down instead of the stairs, mostly because Sheldon and his Coke bottle glasses didn't navigate depth perception well. He'd taken a tumble more than once. Sheldon had a tendency to trip over his own feet on a flat floor.

It was an open-air metal lift that was caged in with bars to keep people and gurneys from falling off. Once it touched ground we stepped off and into my home away from home. The lab was white and sterile, with industrial shelves against one wall and a large walk-in cooler against another. I had a desk with computers and the equipment I used that was certified for forensic use by the state, and it was set up next to my autopsy table.

On the other side of the lab were two embalming tables with built-in drainage, as well as a top-of-the-line ventilation system. Ventilation was important. I didn't really smell any of the usual death scents anymore. I was pretty sure my olfactory senses had been singed at some point. Jack had never gotten a tolerance to the smells of mortuary life. The man could stand in crime scene remnants all day long, but the smell of a little embalming fluid turned him green every time.

Having Lily and Sheldon assist wasn't exactly time efficient. If anything, it would slow me down, but despite human nature having the occasional bent toward evil, victims of homicide didn't come across my table every day. King George was still a small county, and the crime rate was much lower than anywhere around us, so it was good practice for Lily whenever she got the opportunity.

I turned on all the vents and equipment automatically while Sheldon and Lily rolled Juliet from the cooler. The prep work was automatic—mindless activity I'd done countless times before.

Technology had changed things over the last few years. Advancements and computer programs were more efficient, less messy, and less personal. But there was something about human touch that revealed things about what happened to a victim that a computer program would never accomplish. Death, if anything, was personal.

I still liked to handwrite my own notes and make sketches, and then I'd log all my notes into the computer once I was finished. I'd learned from experience that it was always good to have a backup, because technology had a tendency to fail at the exact moment you didn't need it to.

I put the evidence bags on the sterile metal table that flanked my desk, and then put on my lab coat, washed my hands, and gloved up. Any samples I collected from the clothing would have to go to the state crime lab, but getting the samples could be a tedious process, especially since the clothing had been in a dumpster and searching for hair or DNA samples would be like looking for a needle in a haystack.

Lily and Sheldon moved the gurney next to the autopsy table and unzipped the body bag. I was watching out of the corner of my eye, but I trusted Lily and she'd completed all her state certifications to work on the deceased while she'd been interning for me. Effectively, she'd been sworn in as assistant coroner for the county, but she couldn't sign off on any of the paperwork.

I pulled a dark burgundy silk scarf from the evidence bag. It was stiff with dried blood, and there were small particulates from the dumpster adhered to it. I swabbed it so blood comparisons could be made, and looked at it closely for any identifying labels, photographing as I went.

I hung the scarf from one of the shaking racks, and turned it on, the gentle vibrations sending particulates to the tray at the bottom of the rack.

"Oh man," Lily said.

"What is it?" I asked, stopping what I was doing to move to the autopsy table.

"Remaining tissues connecting the head and

spinal column detached during transport," she said.

"I figured it probably would," I told her. "It was barely hanging on. That takes a wicked sharp blade and a good deal of force to sever a head."

"He's strong?" Sheldon asked.

"Maybe," I said. "An adrenaline rush will give some people additional strength. We don't want to build an impression that leads us down a false rabbit hole later on. Don't worry about the head. It'll be easier to work with detached."

I moved back to the table and let Lily document the exterior evaluation of the victim—birthmarks, tattoos, trauma, bruises—every inch of the body had to be looked at.

I pulled out the next article of clothing from an evidence bag. It was a black ankle-length cape lined with velvet. It was also stiff with a good amount of blood, presumably the victim's. That first slash across the throat would've been violent and gruesome, and there would have been nothing he could've done to avoid the arterial spray.

He'd been up close and personal. A crime like this was intimate. The killer had probably used the cape to wipe the blood from his face or eyes. He'd have been wearing gloves too, but they hadn't found any in the dumpster. I didn't have any hope that CSI would be able to pull prints from the hilt, but stranger things had happened.

I hung the cape in one of the larger shaking racks, closed the door and flipped the switch.

"Capes were common outerwear during medieval times," Sheldon said. "And then they became fashionable during the nineteenth century."

"I think that one falls into the latter category," I said. "It's thick and velvet lined. And it has pockets."

"Ooh, pockets," Lily said. "I love it when things have pockets."

I removed the knife from the remaining evidence bag and held it up to the light. It was wicked and sharp, just like I'd mentioned to Sheldon it would have to be.

"That's pretty much my criteria for clothing at this stage of my life," I said. "I want pockets and I need it to feel like pajamas. I don't care if it's loungewear or formal wear."

"Yeah, I'm not there yet," Lily said. "I still like for my shoes to be uncomfortable and sexy and for my clothes to have that look-but-don't-touch vibe."

"I don't know what any of that means," Sheldon said, looking confused.

"It means no matter what a lady is wearing, tell her she looks beautiful and then shut up," Lily said.

"What if she doesn't look beautiful?" he asked.

"Then really make sure you tell her. That's when she needs to hear it most."

"Women are confusing," Sheldon said.

"Men aren't exactly a walk in the park," Lily told him.

Even though there wasn't obvious blood coating

the blade, you could never get rid of it all unless the killer had time to thoroughly clean the knife. I swabbed the blade with a Q-tip and watched the swab turn purple, indicating there was blood present. I found a visible sample in a crevice of the hilt and took a secondary sample to be sent off to the crime lab.

By the time I was finished and had signed off on the paperwork and gathered and labeled all the samples being sent off, Lily and Sheldon had finished prepping Juliet. She lay on the table, her clothes removed and bagged for the state lab to analyze, and her face forever frozen in the gray hues of death.

"She looks sad," Lily said.

I'd been thinking the same thing.

"After talking with her husband earlier, I don't think Juliet was a very happy woman. But she was always looking."

There was pity to be had in deaths like Juliet's. Pity in a young life taken so carelessly. And pity that the man who'd promised to love her didn't mourn. I called out to Alexa to turn on my playlist and Billie Holiday's "Lady Sings the Blues" came over the speakers. It seemed fitting somehow.

"Maybe finding her killer will bring her a little peace in death," I said. "Let's get to work."

We rolled Juliet back into the cooler a little after noon, the autopsy complete. Lily and Sheldon cleaned up in silence. There wasn't anything more we could do for Juliet Dunnegan.

"Well, that was a bummer," Lily said.

"I think I'll pass on the next autopsy," Sheldon said. "I don't really find them that interesting, but I like the embalming process better. When I'm embalming it never feels like the person is staring over my shoulder and watching themselves on the table." He shivered. "I don't think Juliet has completely passed on. I saw a documentary once that said people's souls can hang around for a while after they die, especially if they die traumatically."

"Nonsense," Lily said. "There's no hanging around. My mama always said you've got two options—heaven or hell—so you better choose wisely. The only living things down here are the three of us and that yogurt that's been in the mini-fridge since last summer."

"Did you know that only 61 percent of Americans believes hell is real?" Sheldon asked.

"Doesn't surprise me one bit," I said. "I'm of the school of thought that hell is probably already overcrowded and the population is only going to grow. But my opinion might be skewed based on our line of work and that we get to see the kind of evil that most people never witness."

"Maybe they could get some of those coffin apartments like they have in Tokyo to squeeze more people in."

Neither Lily nor I had a response to that, and I looked down at my phone, grateful to see the message from Jack.

"Jack texted," I told them. "We can meet him and Cole for lunch and tell them what we found."

"You can tell them," Lily said. "I'm going to comfort myself with a daytime margarita."

"The most expensive margarita costs twelve hundred dollars," Sheldon said.

"I'm content with the five-dollar version myself," Lily said. "Taco Joe's has cheap drinks."

"And they have queso," I said. "I call that a winning combination."

"It makes me constipated," Sheldon said.

"Then I would order something else for lunch," I said dryly.

While Lily and Sheldon cleaned up the kitchen, I slipped into my office and changed into a clean pair of jeans and a black sweater, and I found an older pair of black booties toward the back of the closet. I didn't have time for a shower, which was the only thing that would make me feel less covered in death, but it was good enough for Taco Joe's.

"Ready?" I asked, coming back out of the office.

"Black is the color of death and mourning for the ancient Romans," Sheldon said.

"What about modern-day Americans?" I asked as we put on coats and scarves and gloves.

"It means you're bold and confident," he said automatically. "But I don't really understand why. I personally think people just don't know how to match their clothes well and black goes with everything."

I set the alarm and locked the kitchen door, and we loaded up in the Suburban, with Sheldon sitting flat on the bed in the back where the caskets and gurneys slid in.

"This is fine," he said, licking his lips. "I'll be fine. It's a short drive."

I turned on the ignition, checked my rearview, and then backed out of the drive and into the street. As soon as I pressed on the brake, I heard a tumble and an *oomph* as Sheldon made contact with the back door of the Suburban.

"I'm fine," he said, and Lily and I turned in our seats to look back at him. He was half on his knees with his head pressed into the floor mats at an odd angle. His glasses were skewed and the little amount of hair on his head was sticking up in a tuft.

"Maybe brace your legs against the side of the car," Lily said helpfully.

"Good idea," he said, getting into position.

I lost count of how many times Sheldon said he was fine on the drive to Taco Joe's, but by the time we got out of the car he looked like he'd been tossed in the dryer for a couple of hours.

The look on my and Lily's faces must have been alarming because he said, "I'm fine," again, while trying to straighten his clothing.

"Hey, Doc," the hostess said as soon as we

walked through the door. The smell of fresh tortillas and deliciousness assaulted my senses. "Sheriff has a table in the back."

"Thanks, Molly," I said, smiling.

Molly had become a familiar face over the last several months. Ever since Joe and Esme Martinez had opened up Taco Joe's, Jack and I had spent what might be considered an unhealthy amount of time in the corner booth at the back of the restaurant.

"How's Doug?" she asked, her cheeks pinkening slightly.

"He's great," I told her. "Settling in and going to school."

"He likes to come in for happy hour when we do half-priced tortillas," Molly said.

"That doesn't surprise me one bit," I said. "I'm surprised Joe and Esme haven't put a limit on him yet."

She laughed, a tinkling sound that was pure joy and something else. Maybe nerves.

"Oh, they have," she said. "No one can eat like Doug."

"He'll grow into his feet one day," I said.

"Well, tell him to come see me again soon," she said. "Maybe on Wednesday at two. That's when I get off."

"Oh," I said, understanding finally dawning. "Yeah, I'll do that." And then I hurried after Lily and Sheldon to the table where Jack and Cole were waiting for us.

"You have a weird look on your face," Jack said, getting up to greet me.

"How old do you think Molly is?" I asked.

Jack shrugged. "I don't know. I think she's in college. Why?"

"That's what I thought," I said. "She's interested in Doug."

Jack rocked back on his heels. "Our Doug? The Doug who leaves empty pizza boxes on the counter and his dirty socks two feet from the clothes hamper?"

"One and the same," I said. "She wants him to meet her on Wednesday for happy hour. Do you think we should tell her he's only sixteen?"

"Nope," Jack said. "He needs to tell her. I'll talk to him. Though I can't imagine it'd be too hard to figure out."

"Maybe he has some serious game," Cole said, squeezing in next to Lily in the round corner booth.

"I'm going to give you a chance to revise your statement since you've met the Doug we're talking about," Jack said, his lips pressing together.

"You and I both know it's always an older woman who kicks a boy's hormones into full gear," Cole said. "For me it was Mrs. Hanson. Fifth grade. She wore this red sweater that sent me into puberty much too early. Changed my life forever. Besides, I thought nerds were in now. I'm sure Doug gets all the ladies."

"If by ladies you mean his creepy computer,

then you're probably right," I said. "I'm not sure real girls are ready for Doug."

The waiter arrived and said, "I'm Henry. What can I get you to drink?"

"I want a margarita. Lots of salt. Lots of tequila," Lily said.

"Wow," Cole said, surprised. "That must have been one hell of an autopsy."

Henry jostled his notepad at the word *autopsy* and his eyes went wide.

"Don't worry," I told him. "We washed our hands."

Henry didn't look convinced.

"It wasn't one of my favorites," Lily said. "But now it's officially my day off, so drinks."

"Ahh, sometimes I miss my twenties," I said. "When you get our age day drinking is usually followed by heartburn and an immediate need for a nap."

"I'd like to go back to the statement about how this autopsy wasn't one of your favorites," Cole said. "Does that mean you have a favorite?"

"Definitely," Lily said.

"Me too," I followed up. "There are some that just stick with you."

Jack and Cole looked at us like we were crazy, and Sheldon was still perusing the drink menu, not paying attention to the conversation.

"I'll have what she's having," Sheldon finally said. "It's my day off too."

I'd only witnessed Sheldon under the influence

of alcohol once before, and he'd made some pretty terrible decisions that had almost gotten him killed. I was hoping today wasn't going to be like the last time.

Jack must have had the same thought because he looked at me with a combination of amusement and pure terror in his eyes.

"So, did you find anything?" Jack asked, after Henry had disappeared.

"You could say that," I said. "She was pregnant. About sixteen weeks. She wasn't really showing yet."

Jack's mouth went into a hard line. "Double homicide."

"She's not delivered any other children," I said. "She's late thirties, almost forty, and after talking with her husband this morning I have to wonder if it was planned."

"Especially if she's meeting a guy named Peter in the alley late at night," Cole put in. "We found a potential match for him, by the way. Figured we could swing by and talk to him after lunch. His name is Peter Trest. He owns the Curtain Call."

"I've heard of him," I said, but I couldn't remember where I'd heard his name before and I looked at Jack quizzically.

"Trest Art Gallery," Jack said. "And the concert hall over in King George Proper."

Now it clicked. "Got it," I said. "Man's got money."

"And some to spare," Jack agreed.

"I took samples so we can determine paternity," I said. "Everything is in the cooler in the Suburban and ready to send off to the lab. Tox screen came back with Phenergan in her system. She must have still been having issues with morning sickness, which makes sense because she's a little underweight. But if she had a prescription it means she had a doctor, so that's another name to add to the list."

"Anything unusual about the knife wounds?" Jack asked.

The waiter was delivering drinks and chips and salsa and hanging on to every word we were saying. I had a feeling we'd all end up on TikTok if we weren't careful, so I waited until he left again before answering.

"I swabbed the blade so it can be compared to the victim's blood, but the wound looks like a visual match to the knife. Left to right strike, so the killer was right handed, but he didn't just slice the blade across the throat."

Sheldon was sitting next to me so I used him as an example, and turned and faced him like the killer would've been facing Juliet.

"It was a stab wound, not a slice, and he went all the way through the neck tissue and nicked the spinal column." I held my arm up and pretended I was holding a knife, and then I brought it down, showing where the initial strike had been in the side of the neck.

"The first strike is the killing blow," I said. "Not

even immediate medical attention would've saved her. Knife is embedded almost to the hilt, and then he jerks it downward toward her clavicle."

I made a quick motion and Sheldon went pale, sweat dotting his upper lip. I patted him encouragingly on the shoulder.

"And then he did it again," I said. "There's a second entry wound, but the trajectory is different. This cut is almost straight across until it gets to the other side of her neck, and then it tilts up slightly and it's not as deep."

"She was falling to the ground," Jack said.

I could tell he was seeing it fully in his head. Jack had the ability to see a crime scene like no one I'd ever met. He could put himself there and see and understand things that the naked eye couldn't always see. I knew from experience it wasn't always a comfortable gift to live with.

"Exactly," I said. "He would've been covered in blood, but at that point the rage kicked in. She had thirty-seven stab wounds to the chest, many of them going all the way through the torso. If you look at the tip of the knife blade you can see where the point is broken off either from where it hit pavement or bone."

"Serious rage," Cole said. "That kind of close-contact anger usually means the killer and victim knew each other. What could make someone so angry that they'd mutilate a pregnant woman?"

"Maybe a husband who didn't like that his wife's baby belonged to another man," Jack said.

"Or a lover who didn't want to be saddled with child support for the next eighteen years," Lily chimed in. "There are lots of variables when husbands and lovers come into play."

"They generally don't mix well," I said.

Jack's lips twitched. "So noted for future reference."

I pressed my lips together. "Anyway," I said, arching a brow at Jack, "After the frenzy the killer must have realized he was taking too big of a risk. It was then he dragged her behind the dumpster and gutted her. Everything he did after the initial strike to the neck was all postmortem."

"He's like Jack the Ripper," Sheldon said offhandedly, licking at the salt around his glass.

Everyone got quiet and stared at him, including Henry, who'd inched his way back to refill drinks that were already full.

Sheldon looked back at each of us nervously, his eyes blinking owlishly behind the lenses of his glasses. "What?" he asked.

Jack stared at Henry until he finally got the hint and moved away. "What do you mean he's like Jack the Ripper?"

Sheldon sat up straight and I could tell by the expression on his face he was about to go into lecture mode.

"You've never heard of Jack the Ripper?" Sheldon asked. "I thought he would be considered notorious in your line of work."

"I've heard of Jack the Ripper," Jack said

patiently. "I want to know why our current killer is like him."

"Oh," Sheldon said. "That makes more sense. Jack the Ripper wreaked havoc across Whitechapel in London in 1888. He was believed to be responsible for the deaths of eleven women—all of them women of ill repute."

"Ill repute?" Lily asked.

Sheldon blushed. "You know what I mean." And then he lowered his voice to a whisper. "Ladies of the night." He cleared his throat awkwardly and took another fortifying drink. "He sliced their throats and eventually disemboweled them. Did you know disembowelment became a popular brand of torture in the thirteenth century, usually for reasons of treason against the king? Very messy, but effective."

"Even the clothing played into the scenario," Cole said.

"So he just waited for the right moment to fulfill a fantasy?" I asked.

"It makes sense in a twisted way," Jack said. "Newcastle looks like Victorian England. The costumes are right. And he picks a victim who he considers to be a woman of ill repute. If the killer did any research at all he'd know how Jack the Ripper killed his victims."

"Now we just have to hope he doesn't do it again," Lily said, shivering.

"Last night was the end of the Victorian festival," I said. "Maybe she's an isolated incident. We know he was dressed well. The items of clothing retrieved from the dumpster were a silk scarf and a cape. They were both good quality. Formal and meant for a night out on the town.”

“Like at the theater?” Cole asked. “Do they keep records of ticket purchases? Killer goes to see her perform, strolls out of the theater looking like all the other attendees, and then slips around to the alley while everyone goes to watch the fireworks.”

“The common theme I keep getting from this is theater,” I said. “Not just the location and costumes and that, according to Juliet’s husband, she liked being the star of her own show. But now we have the possibility that Peter Trest is Juliet’s lover. He owns the theater and has access to high-quality costumes.”

“It sounds like we need to go talk to Peter Trest,” Jack said.

CHAPTER FIVE

Jack put a call in to his secretary while we finished lunch so she could work on tracking down Peter Trest. Betsy Clement had been a sheriff's secretary for the last forty years, and she'd managed to keep her job through good sheriffs and bad ones. She knew just about everyone, and if she didn't know them, she probably knew something about them or their family. She kept secrets better than the Illuminati and she was nosier than a bloodhound after a scent. If you wanted something to get done, you called Betsy Clement.

"Any luck?" I asked Jack.

We gathered our coats and things and stood in the foyer, waiting for Lily to get out of the bathroom. I looked out at the gloomy weather, wishing for even a glimpse of sun, but there was nothing but gray skies and the distorted view of the world through the rain.

"Didn't even take her five minutes to track him

down," Jack said. "He'll meet us at his gallery office in Newcastle. You want to handle it solo or do you want company?"

Jack was always respectful to give his detectives the authority to work cases how they wanted to, but all his detectives respected Jack enough to know he had skills they might never have.

Cole sighed. "Martinez just texted. Can you and Doc handle Trest? A potential witness just came into the station. I guess the media has finally gotten hold of this and he heard it on the news. According to Martinez, the witness says he saw a guy with blood on his shirt and acting strange before the fireworks started. I'm going to call in Samson and see if we can get a sketch started so we can get it circulated. Maybe we'll get lucky right out of the gate."

Samson was the sketch artist, and I had no idea how he'd gotten the nickname Samson since he was only a few inches over five feet and maybe weighed a hundred and twenty pounds soaking wet.

"Why do they call him Samson?" Sheldon asked, hiccupping lightly. His eyes were glazed and he always looked slightly rumpled, but somehow our hour at lunch sitting in a booth was the equivalent of him looking like he'd spent a week at Mardi Gras.

"Because his name is Samson," Cole said.

I was suddenly glad I hadn't voiced my curiosity. "That's kind of a letdown. I thought there'd be a great story as to why everyone called him that."

"I think it was wishful thinking on his parents' part," Jack said.

Lily came out of the bathroom zipping her coat and wrapping a colorful scarf around her neck. One margarita was no match for Lily. She looked alert and vibrant and like she'd spent the last hour sipping tea.

"What'd I miss?" she asked.

"Samson isn't a nickname," Sheldon said. "It's his real name."

"That's kind of a bummer," Lily said. "You don't look so good. How many margaritas did you have?"

"Just the one," he said. "And then I think I might have accidentally drank some of yours. I got nervous after Doc pretended to kill me."

"Understandable," Lily said. "Don't throw up in the car. I remember you having a much higher tolerance for alcohol."

"I'm out of practice," Sheldon said. "I lost the desire to drink after we went to that mortuary conference and that woman tied me to the bed and then murdered a bunch of people. Mother said I should keep a clear head where women are concerned, but I figured I was fine around you and Doc. Y'all aren't like regular women."

"Amen," Jack said.

"I'll make sure you get home," Lily said, patting Sheldon on the back gently.

"I can't go home on blackjack Bible study days," he said, looking pitiful.

"It's not over yet?" I asked, looking at the time on my phone.

"Oh, no," Sheldon said. "It's a tournament. It won't be done until midnight. Mama likes to preach between rounds."

I wished I could say that blackjack Bible study was the strangest thing I'd ever heard happening, but it wasn't even in the top ten. The people in King George County were a different kind of people.

I tossed Lily the keys to the Suburban. "You rode in with Cole," I reminded her. "You don't have a vehicle."

"I'll leave it under the portico and drive Sheldon's car to my place. He can sleep on the couch."

"My place is closer," Cole said. "Just take him there. You know where everything is. Just make yourself at home. You've got a key. I might even make it home tonight if this witness plays out."

Lily's smile was seductive and she moved in close to Cole. "I like the sound of that."

My eyebrows rose to my hairline and I felt Jack's hand on the back of my neck, squeezing ever so slightly. I had questions. A lot of questions. Cole had always been very proprietary about his house. And now to find out Lily had a key. That was big news.

I'd never been one to be big on gossip, mostly because I'd spent most of my life being gossiped about. But Lily was my friend, and I was straddling the line between being nosy and wanting to make sure she was protected in case things went bad with Cole.

"We're out," Jack said, putting his hand on the small of my back and ushering me toward the door. "We'll let you know how it goes with Trest."

Jack and I hurried and left while Lily and Cole finished saying their goodbyes.

"Other people's love is kind of gross," I said, fastening my seat belt. "Do you think we were that gross when we started dating?"

"Definitely not," he said. "And we didn't really date. We just came to our senses."

"Do you think we should check on Doug?" I asked. "He's still a teenaged boy in a house alone."

"I texted him," Jack said. "He said he ordered pizza and is doing an assignment for class. Then he asked if he could make some modifications to the golf cart."

"What did you tell him?"

"I told him to go ahead, and while he was at it to see if he could amp up the riding lawn mower."

The whole parenting thing was new to me, and parenting a teenager was like jumping into the deep end of the pool when you didn't know how to swim. Doug wasn't a normal kid. I knew the reason he was with us was because we could give him opportunities to stretch his mind without too much fear of going to prison or being reprimanded—within reason.

"Just remember I draw the line at robots," I said.

"The second the toaster starts walking across the counter I'm burning the house to the ground and we're starting over somewhere else."

"I've reminded him," Jack said, driving past the Newcastle city limits sign. "No robots. Newcastle has always been a little creepy to me."

"It's a cute town," I said. "Very artsy. Bloody Mary has a lot of the Tudor influence with a touch of Americana. King George Proper looks like every college town in America, and Nottingham has no style at all. Newcastle has done a good job at revitalizing the city. Art galleries, cafes and bistros, the theater, and all those indie clothing shops where they sell angora and hand-sewn leather and you have to put one of your children up for collateral to purchase anything."

"It's bougie," Jack said.

"You're so hip with the lingo," I said, cracking a smile.

"Doug is teaching me all kinds of words. He says it's the least he can do to pay us back for having a bottomless pantry."

"He realizes that someone actually has to fill the pantry up, right? He doesn't think that it's a magical doorway where elves make sure he never runs out of Soft Batch cookies?"

"Which is why he's going to start doing the grocery shopping every week," Jack said. "I figure now that he's settled in it's time for him to start taking on some responsibilities."

"You're going to be a good dad," I said.

"You say that as if you don't believe you're going to be a good mom."

I shrugged, trying not to think too much about it. We'd been talking about children for the last couple of months. Jack had become comfortable easing into that part of our future. I wasn't there yet. It's not that I didn't want to have children. It's just that my role models for parenthood had been subpar at best, and it was a heavy responsibility to think that I could screw up a couple of more people's lives like my parents had screwed up mine —at least the first part. Not that I was planning to turn to a life of crime and bad decisions anytime soon, but you only know what you know.

Jack was thinking of responsibilities and things that would make Doug grow as a person, and I was thinking that I didn't want to get murdered by a toaster robot in my sleep.

"All I mean is that you're just good at the responsible stuff," I said. "Like giving Doug chores and things like that. I don't know how you can throw yourself into work like you do, and still have the brain capacity to remember to make sure we feed the kids, or put them to bed on time, or pack lunches. When I'm working I have trouble focusing on anything but work. What if I forget to pick up Sally from dance class or leave crime scene photos on the dining room table and traumatize her forever?"

"I'm going to have to put a hard stop on the

name Sally," Jack said. "Sally Lawson clearly works as a barmaid at the saloon on Bonanza."

"You know what I mean," I said, rolling my eyes.

Jack reached over and grabbed my hand, squeezing it firmly. "I want to remind you that you are not your parents. You're not even related to them by blood. But what you are is compassionate and caring, not only toward those who are privileged to be part of your life, but to those who can't speak because their life has ended."

"So I know without a doubt in my mind that when we're ready to bring children into this world that you're going to take care of them and love them and comfort them like you do for all of us. We're both going to make mistakes, but we're going to make them together. That's why there's two of us. We make each other stronger. Where I'm weak, you're strong. And where you're weak, I'm strong. That's what marriage is. We'll screw up together. And we're going to have victories together. But it's all going to be done together."

I squeezed his hand back, but there was something caught in my throat that left me unable to speak. I knew he spoke the truth. Jack had always been the calm in my storms. Did I believe I would be a natural at parenting? No, not at all. But I believed in Jack. And he believed in us. That was good enough for me.

I cleared my throat and blinked the tears from my eyes. "I love you."

Jack winked and said, "I know. I'm very loveable. I'll show you later."

I laughed and shook my head, feeling the tension release from my shoulders.

Now that the festival was over, they'd moved the barriers and let vehicles downtown again. Traffic was light because most businesses on the square were closed Mondays, hardly anyone wanted to be out in weather like this, and because a lot of people were probably recovering after a week of drinking mulled cider and beer.

Jack parked directly in front of Trest Gallery, and I noticed there was a sign on the door that said they were only open by appointments on Monday.

"I'm having trouble placing Trest," I said. "I don't think I've ever met him, but his name is familiar."

Jack nodded. "He donated to the campaign, but he rarely comes to public functions. He's kind of eccentric. When he shows up it's usually last minute or unannounced. Sometimes he'll donate a bunch of money to whatever catches his interest and sometimes he'll leave a thousand-dollar tip at a restaurant. But he mostly keeps to himself."

The front of the gallery was a long stretch of glass windows, and local artists' works were displayed under expensive lighting—everything from more traditional paint on canvas to knitted afghans and sculptures and pieces of furniture. Jack held open the door for me and I was immediately aware of the fact that my casual attire of jeans and sweater did not belong, but I still felt oddly comfortable.

The inside was set up to look more like a house than a gallery, and I found it made me really look at the possibility of each piece instead of trying to figure out some hidden meaning. Though there were some I'd never understand even with a written description.

"Holy Moses," I whispered. "Do you see the price tags on these things? Where do people get that kind of money?"

"All kinds of places," Jack said. "Places like these try to appeal to the bigger cities too so they'll come here to shop."

"As long as they don't move here," I said. "I kind of like that one of the circling fish. Compared to some of the other stuff it seems pretty straight-forward."

"I'm pretty sure those are sperm," Jack said, pressing his thumb and forefinger to the bridge of his nose to keep from laughing.

"How are you getting sperm out of that?" I asked, squinting so I could see better.

"Because it's titled *Sperm Count*. And that's not a boat they're circling."

"Huh," I said. "Good thing I didn't buy it for your office."

Heels clicking against the tile interrupted our conversation and we looked around for the source.

"Sheriff Lawson?" a woman asked, her smile polite.

Her skin was the color of dark caramel, and she had stunning pale blue eyes. Her hair was bleached blond and cut close to the scalp and her features were sharp and pixie-like. She wore a black body-suit with a metallic mesh sarong tied at her waist, and silver stilettos that made my arches ache.

"I'm Lina, Pete's assistant here at the gallery," she said, holding out a narrow hand.

"Nice to meet you," Jack said, shaking her hand. "This is Dr. Graves. We appreciate the time."

She smiled again and said, "Just let me lock up and I'll take you to his studio. He's been up working all night, so he's a little scattered."

Lina locked the front door and then led us to a black door marked *Staff Only*, and then she typed in a code and opened the door. She led us up a set of stairs, and I narrowed my eyes at her perfect behind as we went up because I'd seen the elevator at the end of the hall. I felt Jack's hand pat my backside, giving me a little push as we went up. I could practically hear his laughter. He knew me well. There were two kinds of women in the world—ones who took the elevator and ones who took the stairs. I fell firmly into the elevator camp.

I'd been blessed by good genetics, a slim build, and good cheekbones—probably due to the fact that my birth mother was French—but I'd never had to be too concerned about my diet. I liked caffeine and pastries and bread and wine, so I figured I'd enjoy them until I couldn't any longer.

I was happy that I wasn't winded by the time we

reached the landing at the top of the stairs, but I figured that had more to do with Jack getting me out to walk our property along the cliffs when the weather was nice than anything else.

The first thing I noticed was the light. Two sides of the top floor were nothing but windows, and it had a spectacular view of downtown. I could even see part of the theater from here. The second thing I noticed was the smell—turpentine, paint, and sawdust made my eyes water. The wood floors were scarred and paint splattered, and canvases lined the walls. Instead of a desk, there was a long oak table that was covered in papers and blueprints. Books lined the shelves along the back wall and there were weights and a couple of machines in the far corner.

The space said a lot about the man, and what it told me was that Peter Trest seemed to be a Renaissance man of sorts. He was also interesting to look at.

I'd gotten spoiled by Jack. Most men didn't have his God-given looks, but Jack also had a charisma about him—a quality that drew people to him like bees to honey. I couldn't remember the last time I was in a room with someone more magnetic than Jack. But Peter Trest ran a close second.

He smiled, wiping his hands on an old towel, obviously having just finished washing them. He wore tattered, paint-spattered jeans, and an old denim shirt rolled up to the elbows, showing muscular forearms. His silver hair came down to the top of his shoulders and his brows were thick and dark.

"Thank you, Lina," Trest said. "Sheriff, good to see you again. I wasn't expecting to see you at my door. Lina mentioned a detective."

"Detective Cole got a call and couldn't make it, so I told him I'd pinch-hit. This is Dr. Graves," Jack said, introducing me.

Trest turned his attention toward me, and it felt like he was absorbing all of my features and analyzing them. It was an extremely uncomfortable feeling.

"Fabulous bone structure," he said. "I'd love to paint you."

"No thank you," I said automatically and he laughed out loud.

"She's blunt," Trest said, looking at Jack. "I like that."

"Me too," Jack said. "That's why I married her."

"I apologize," Trest said, his attention back on me. "It's the plight of the artist. Everything and everyone we look at is a subject. But you really are strikingly beautiful. I'm Pete. That's what most everyone calls me."

I was even more uncomfortable with compliments than I was at being stared at, so I said, "Nice to meet you," and then let the silence hang awkwardly.

"Thanks, Lina," Trest said. "We should be good. Could you order lunch for me? I don't think I've eaten since yesterday. Maybe day before that. I get caught up." He shrugged sheepishly and pointed to a large canvas at the other end of the room. It was a cacophony of color and texture—slashes of red and pink and orange and yellow—and it was highly sexual in nature even though I wasn't exactly sure what I was looking at.

"Do you want any water or coffee?" Lina asked us.

"Oh, I should've thought to offer," Trest said. "My brain tends to leave me when I've been in a work fog."

"We're fine," Jack said.

Lina nodded and headed back down the stairs, leaving us alone with Trest.

"You've been here the last two days?" Jack asked. "You slept here?"

Trest put his hands on his hips and looked up, trying to recall. "I came in Saturday afternoon to do some paperwork." He pointed at the table full of papers. "Obviously I didn't get any work done. Sometimes it hits like that. I took a couple of naps on the couch to recharge, but I haven't left the building since then. What's going on? I figured someone was coming to talk to me about fundraising again for the sheriff's office."

"We're not here about fundraising," Jack said. "We wanted to talk to you about Juliet Dunnegan."

Trest looked sheepish again and his smile was half guilty, half scoundrel. "Well, if you're here about Juliet then I'm guessing you already know we have a relationship of sorts. Come on and let's sit down. The adrenaline rush of finishing the painting is fading fast and I'll crash soon."

He led us over to a couch and a couple of straight-backed chairs—he sat in one of the chairs.

"If I sit on the couch I'll fall asleep and you won't get any answers to your questions," he said good-naturedly.

I could see the exhaustion in the lines of his face now, and he had a lazy, contented look to him —not at all like someone who'd just murdered his lover.

"We won't take up much of your time," Jack said.

"It's no trouble," he said. "Really. I've been meaning to maneuver a meeting with you and your wife. I've read about you in the papers."

"Not always the best source of information," I said, thinking of Floyd Parker.

Trest laughed and said, "Definitely not. I've had more than one go-around with them. I always take the motto of using them when you can and ignoring them the rest of the time."

"That's a good motto," I said. "Why did you want to meet with us?" I was curious, and I knew Jack was watching him closely. It seemed unlikely to me that no one had mentioned that someone had been murdered in the alley behind a theater he owned. Not to mention the victim was his lover. But stranger things had happened.

"My art has started to take off," he said. "I'd started it as a hobby—a way to blow off steam and relax outside of the business world. But galleries have started buying pieces on commission and I've been asked to do a show in London next fall. I'm always looking for inspiration. I did an entire series on life, beginning with conception. You might have seen some of those paintings downstairs."

I nodded politely and prayed he didn't want me to contribute to the conversation, especially since it had looked like nothing more than a school of fish and a boat. I clearly didn't have an artistic eye.

"It's been very popular," he said. "I was hoping to do a complementary series on death. I thought you might share some of your darker cases. Or nightmares even."

There was a morbid curiosity in his question that was unsettling, but Jack had said Trest was eccentric.

"Please don't think me gruesome," he said as if reading my mind. He smiled again, totally at ease with himself, and he ran his fingers through his hair. "I find that dreams and nightmares give some of the best inspiration for what I put on canvas."

"I don't dream," I told Trest.

"Never?" he asked.

"Never," I lied.

"Interesting," he said. "It almost seems unnatural. Maybe you should try hypnosis and see if you can unlock your subconscious."

The thought terrified me. I'd done a lot of healing over the last couple of years. I'd be damned if I purposefully took myself back to those dark places.

"It's probably best it stay locked," I said, firmly.

"There was a murder in the alley behind your theater last night," Jack said. "I thought you might have been notified already."

"What?" Trest asked, leaning forward in his chair. "What happened? I haven't had the TV on in days, and Lina knows not to bother me unless it's an emergency." He looked back and forth between the two of us. "I guess this counts as an emergency. When she came up to check on me this morning she just happened to catch me at the end of my work. I didn't put it together when she told me the detective wanted to meet with me."

"It happened sometime after midnight," Jack told him. "The theater had just let out and everyone was distracted by the fireworks."

"That's terrible," he said, his gaze wandering out the window toward the park. I wasn't sure whether it was exhaustion or he was a space cadet, but he didn't seem to be able to focus well. "They were beautiful fireworks. I think it's what gave me an added boost of inspiration to push through to the finish."

His head jerked, as if he were coming back into himself and he said, "Wait a minute. You said you wanted to talk to me about Juliet. Why would you say that?"

"Juliet Dunnegan is our victim," Jack said, and I watched as Trest's face went pale with shock.

"That can't be possible," he said. "We were supposed to meet. Tonight, I think. What day is this?"

"Monday," I said.

He closed his eyes and let out a slow, measured breath. "Last night. We were supposed to meet last night after the performance. She was supposed to stop by and we were going to watch the fireworks from here together."

"When was the last time you talked to Juliet?" Jack asked.

"I don't know," he said, shrugging. "Sometime last week. We both get busy. She was doing the play all week, so it was before that when we made plans. A week ago, I guess. She stayed the night at my place and then had to be at the theater early the next morning. I told her on closing night to meet me here for fireworks." He laughed to himself, but there was no joy in the laughter. "Double entendre intended."

"How long had you and Juliet been seeing each other?" Jack asked.

Trest looked at Jack and asked, "Are you sure it's her? It just doesn't seem possible. I mean, Juliet is so full of life."

"Someone ended her life for her," Jack said. "It's up to us to find who did this to her."

"Her husband," Trest said automatically. "He's a real piece of work. Rigid. Controlling. He never understood Juliet."

"You two have issues?" Jack asked.

"We've never met," Trest said. "He knew about us though. Juliet told me he knew. I try not to get into people's personal business. If it had bothered Juliet too much she would've broken things off and I would've stepped back. It wasn't a big deal. We had fun with each other. She's a creative too. Very passionate about her work. High drama. It makes sense that we were attracted to each other. It was fireworks all the time. From fighting to making love. It fueled both of our work."

"Did her husband ever threaten her?" Jack asked.

"Juliet always said his bark was worse than his bite. He threatened to cut her off a time or two, but they've been married a while and from what I understand he's pretty successful at whatever he does. She would've walked away with a sweet deal if he'd divorced her."

"It doesn't sound like you know much about her," I said.

"Well," he said, his grin attempting to be charming. "I know her very well in some ways. But we didn't have that kind of relationship. We had sex. It was fun. And it would've eventually ended with no harm, no foul. It's not like she would've left her husband for me, and I have no plans to ever get in a long-term relationship. She could've had other lovers for all I know. I wasn't exclusively seeing Juliet either. We hooked up when it was convenient with our schedules."

"She was four months pregnant," Jack said. "Did she happen to mention that?"

I thought he might be sick. His lips went white and he tried to get to his feet, but he stumbled and caught himself on the coffee table.

"Mr. Trest," I said, coming to my feet in case he was going into cardiac arrest. "Take some deep breaths for me."

He tried to stand again and his chair toppled over backward. This time he just let himself go to his knees on the floor.

His mouth moved wordlessly and I looked at Jack, concerned we might need to call an ambulance.

"Pete," Jack said. "Do you need medical attention?"

"Imposs…impossible," he croaked out. "It's impossible. Juliet couldn't have children."

"Sometimes the impossible happens," I said, softly. "If you'd like to do a paternity test we can see if the baby was yours."

He nodded wordlessly. "Yes," he said. "Yes, I'd like to know for sure. I don't know what else to say."

"You can think back over the last several weeks," Jack said. "Conversations you and Juliet might have had. Someone targeted her. They sent her flowers and signed your name. She thought she was going out in the alley to meet you. Do you have a record of everyone who buys tickets for the show?"

"It's done through the website," he said. "If they

paid online there's a record. They can pay cash at the box office. We don't keep record of those."

"Do you have cameras at the box office?" Jack asked.

Trest licked his lips and looked around, as if wondering how he'd ended up on the floor. "Yes," he said. "We have one inside the box office and outside since we take cash. She thought she was meeting me? Pregnant."

"We're going to find out who did this to her."

"I never wanted children," he said. "But somehow it feels different to think of it as mine. I'll do whatever I can to help you. But I think I need to be alone for a little while."

"We're very sorry for your loss," Jack said.

"It's loss that makes art great," he said. "That's what I'll hold on to."

CHAPTER SIX

"WHAT WAS YOUR INITIAL IMPRESSION?" JACK ASKED after we'd gotten back in the car.

"My initial impression?" My lips twitched, and I glanced at him. "He's got a magnetic personality. Like you. He knows how to work a room. Perform. But he's selfish at the core. I don't like him."

Jack barked out a laugh. "Tell me how you really feel."

"Hey, you asked!"

"You're right," he said. "I've met him a couple of times before, but never talked to him for long. But I'm in agreement with you. I don't like him either. There's something off there."

"Maybe it's the narcissism," I said dryly. "Do you think he could've done it?"

"Anyone can kill someone depending on the situation," Jack said. "We both know that well enough. But as to whether he murdered Juliet, I don't know. He could've been acting. Or he could've been so self-absorbed in his painting that he really didn't notice she never showed up like she was supposed. I definitely don't think he knew about the baby."

"No, I don't think so either," I said. "How old do you think he is?"

"Mid-fifties, maybe? Probably around the same age as her husband." Jack did a U-turn in the street. "Let's head over to the theater and see if anyone is there. Let's see what the security cameras have to say."

There were still blockades up leading into the alley, but the patrol cars were gone since the scene had been cleared. Jack flipped on his lights and parked right in front of the theater.

"I don't see anyone," I said, looking in through the glass doors.

Jack knocked and we waited a few seconds. "I can have Betsy call the manager and get someone here to get it open for us. We'll need a warrant for all the credit card purchases anyway."

We were just turning away when a face appeared in the glass. Jack held up his badge and the harried man nodded and unlocked the door.

"I thought you were more reporters," he said, ushering us inside. "I was about to give you a piece of my mind."

"I'm glad you didn't," Jack said, putting the guy at ease, and then he held out his hand and introduced himself. "Sheriff Lawson."

"Rick Early," the guy said, shaking Jack's hand.

He was a couple of inches shorter than Jack and thinner through the shoulders and hips. He had freshly cut blond hair and his face was shaved smooth. His eyes were pale gray and intelligent, and his jeans and sweater crisply pressed.

"I'm the theater manager," he said. "The police told me I could finally come inside about an hour ago. We were supposed to tear everything down this morning and all the actors were supposed to clean out their dressing rooms. We've got rehearsals starting tomorrow for the next show. Or they're supposed to start tomorrow. I think we're going to have to delay. I've been trying to call Mr. Trest, but I haven't been able to get through."

"We just came from there," Jack said. "He told us you've got cameras in the box office. Could we take a look at those?"

"Oh, yeah," Rick said. "Sure. Security room is right over here. It's kind of small."

"How long is the feed recorded?" Jack asked.

Rick unlocked a gray utilitarian door and propped it open. "It recycles automatically after seventy-two hours."

"Are there cameras in the alley?" I asked.

"Unfortunately, no," Rick said. "Mr. Trest just focuses on the trafficked areas or where we keep money. We had an employee walk off with all the cash once, so that's when the cameras were installed. I guess you never think you'll have to worry too much about this kind of stuff in a place like Newcastle."

"Can I see the feed for yesterday?" Jack asked.

"Sure," Rick said. "I can pull it up. I'll make you copies of the last three days to take with you."

"I appreciate the help," Jack said.

"Oh, sure," Rick said. "It's no trouble. We all want you to catch this guy. Everyone knew Juliet."

That caught my attention. "Did you know her well?"

"Not really," Rick said, his eyes focused on the monitor in front of him. "But I'm not sure anyone really did. She was kind of one of those women who was always at the center of attention, but still seemed kind of lonely. Maybe Mr. Trest knew her better than anyone. Or Dan. He's the director here, and Juliet has been in a lot of his productions."

"You knew about Juliet's relationship with Peter Trest?" Jack asked.

"Oh, sure," Rick said, fast-forwarding through the feed and slowing it down every time someone bought tickets. "I don't think it was a secret though. They never bothered to hide their relationship."

"What about Juliet's husband?" I asked. "Did he ever come up here?"

Rick's eyebrows rose and he stared at us in surprise. "She was married?"

"Yes," Jack said.

"Wow, I had no idea," he said, shaking his head. "I thought she was as single as they come. She's always dated around, you know."

"Wait a second," Jack said, leaning toward the monitor. "Let's get a look at that guy."

"Look at the cape," I said, moving in closer. "Could be him. He's tall."

"Is there a way to get a clearer shot of his face?" Jack asked. "A different angle? The top hat is blocking the view."

"Maybe," Rick said, bringing up another camera. "These are the only two cameras."

"He knows about the cameras," Jack said, watching him. "His hat is tilted to cover most of his face, and he's making sure to stay still."

"You can see a partial of his jaw," I said. "Maybe Carver can get a better image."

"I doubt it," Jack said. "You can't make something out of nothing." Then he asked Rick, "Could you make me a list of anyone who had a relationship with Juliet in the past? Maybe someone didn't want to be jilted."

"Sure, I can do that," he said. "I can only think of a few anyway, but like I said, talk to Dan. He might be able to add a few more names to the list."

We got a copy of the security feed and a short list of names, and we said our goodbyes to Rick Early.

"I'll drop you at the funeral home and then meet up with Cole to fill him in," Jack said.

"I'm going to go ahead and go home," I said. "I've got nothing left to do at the funeral home, and I can start setting up the murder board and running some of the names on the list Rick gave us."

"Sounds like a plan," Jack said. "Maybe invite Carver and Michelle to dinner."

"Do I have to cook?" I asked.

"God no," Jack said, looking horrified. "Carver's been through enough. We can order in."

"I could learn to cook one day," I said defensively.

"I'm not so sure about that," Jack said. "I've seen you try to follow a recipe. We all have gifts. And yours is not in the kitchen."

"That's not what you said a couple of weeks ago," I said, cutting my eyes toward him.

He grinned. "I stand corrected. You're amazing in the kitchen as long as you don't cook anything."

I was mildly satisfied with that answer.

"I won't be too late unless something comes up," Jack said, pulling in behind the Suburban.

I was surprised to see it was already after four. "We still haven't told Brian Dunnegan Juliet was pregnant."

"I'll tell him," Jack said. "I've got to call and let him know her body will be released to him tomorrow."

"Better you than me," I said, giving him a quick kiss goodbye. "See you at home."

Three hours later, I found myself alone in the house and enjoying the solitude. I was an introvert by nature, and unless I had to be out, I preferred to be home. It was one of the reasons I loved working with the dead—they never talked back.

Jack was the complete opposite. He thrived when he was surrounded by people and the more conversations he had, the more energized he was. I could mostly overlook that flaw in him because he brought me coffee in bed every morning and the sex was incredible.

Dinner with the Carvers had been a bust. Carver said they were neck deep in unpacking, but I wasn't sure I was buying it. Something in his voice had been off. And Doug had decided to head off to the movies with a friend. When the friend had pulled up in the driveway, he'd bounded down the stairs, yelled goodbye over his shoulder, and shut the front door behind him before I could say a word. I had managed to get a glimpse of a cute blonde behind the wheel of a red Jeep before they'd driven off.

I decided to switch to tea and put on the kettle to boil while I went in the office and started setting up the murder board. I was a visual person, so seeing faces and names laid out was a huge help to organize my thoughts. And it helped that Jack's office was equipped with some of the best technology in existence, mostly thanks to Carver.

The whiteboard that took up an entire wall was like a giant computer screen. With just a few simple commands Juliet's picture showed in the middle of the board—it was a headshot she used for the programs from the theater. She was a beautiful woman and the way she looked into the camera spoke of confidence and independence.

The photograph next to the headshot was one taken at the crime scene. Gone was the vivaciousness of life, and in its place was the blank, cloudy stare of death. The rage in the attack was obvious. But he'd left her face untouched and only mutilated her body.

I thought back to what Sheldon had said about Jack the Ripper and did an internet search. The good thing about it was that he was such a notorious killer that all of the information about each of the crimes was online—crime scene photographs, evidence pictures, testimony. It was all available at the touch of a fingertip. The bad thing about it was that there'd been numerous copycats over the last century or so.

I used a section of the board to post the old crime scene photographs, lining them up in the order each victim had been found. There were similarities. Throats slit. Multiple stab wounds. And none of them had been sexually assaulted.

"But you got carried away," I said, staring at the photograph of Juliet. "Jack the Ripper killed for sport." I looked at the old photographs again, closer this time. "He picked his victims and did the job. The murders were almost clinical in a way. They even thought he might have been a doctor. But you were beyond mad. In a rage. You were really angry at Juliet."

Something scraped against the windows and I

jumped. The wind had picked up and I could hear the rain. "Just a branch," I whispered, but just in case I moved behind Jack's desk and took the revolver out of the drawer, laying it on the desk.

I checked my phone, but there were no messages from Jack except for his last text that he'd be later than he thought. And then the whistle blew from the kettle and I let out a screech.

"Good grief," I said, my heart racing. "Get a grip."

I was alone with dead bodies on a daily basis and I was letting a tree branch and a teakettle get to me. I wiped my sweaty palms on my jeans, grabbed the gun, and brought it into the kitchen with me. I tried to ignore the fact that the house had an inordinate amount of windows, and that it felt like eyes were watching me from the outside.

I knew what it felt like to be attacked in the place you should feel safest. I'd been there before, and I struggled to keep the memories at bay of what it felt like to be helpless against someone stronger. Jack made me feel safe, and I'd gradually let my guard down over the last couple of years.

Jack had taken precautions with our home—installing perimeter cameras, a high-tech security system, and a gate at the end of our driveway. I was safe. None of the alarms had been triggered.

I put the gun on the counter and poured hot water over tea leaves, adding milk and sugar, and then I defiantly looked out the windows and into the darkness.

"No one is there," I said aloud. "And if there is I will shoot the hell out of them." I added that last part just in case there *was* someone there and they read lips.

I was stepping out of the kitchen and back across the hall to the office when the front door opened. Hot liquid sloshed across my hand, but it barely registered as I started to bring the gun up.

"Hey there," Jack said, standing very still in the open doorway. The porch light shone behind him, magnifying the rain, and he was soaked through to the skin. "Everything okay?"

"I'm fine," I said, lowering the gun and blowing out a shaky breath. "I just let my imagination get the best of me."

He came all the way in and closed the door behind him, acting as if nothing was out of the ordinary so I could get myself together. But he put the deadbolt on and reset the alarm before hanging his coat on the hook.

I was just starting to feel the sting of the hot water now that my heartrate was slowing, and I turned and walked back into the kitchen and straight to the sink.

Jack came up behind me and put his arms around me, looking over my shoulder at the pink skin on the top of my hand. He lifted my hand and brought it to his mouth, kissing it gently.

"I'm sorry you were scared," he said.

"Like I said, I just let my imagination get the best of me with the sounds from the storm and being home alone. I know I'm safe here. I *feel* safe here," I assured him.

"Home alone," he said. "Where's Doug?"

"He went to a movie with someone named Tamara," I said. "I told him he needs to be back by eleven."

Jack turned me in his arms so I faced him, and I could see his smile. "Look at you with your curfews. How very parental of you."

"It caught me by surprise too," I said. "But it's Monday night in Bloody Mary. Once the movie is over there's nothing left to do."

"Which shows you've never been a teenage boy," he said.

"Why are you so late?" I asked. "What happened?"

"When I came into the station Cole and Samson were still working with the witness. His name is Guy Carolla. Guy said he was heading south from his apartment down Danbury toward the park. He was meeting friends to watch the fireworks, and this man comes stumbling toward him. Guy thought he was drunk, but as he got closer he thought maybe he'd been hurt or robbed. The man was using a cane, and his arm was across his stomach with his hand hidden under his jacket. There was blood on his shirt."

"Did the witness see his face?" I asked.

"It was partially hidden by a top hat, and Guy said he had a goofy-looking mustache. Probably a fake. So he didn't get a good look at the eyes. Just an impression of a nose and the jawline. But we know he's Caucasian, and a little over six feet since Guy said the man was taller than he was. Top hat matches what we saw from the security camera. He was in formal attire, which makes sense if he'd watched the performance at the theater."

"Danbury Street," I said, narrowing my eyes. "That's where Trest's Art Gallery is."

"I know," Jack said. "So Cole and I went back out and walked the area like Guy described, and we timed how long of a walk it was from the alley behind the theater to where Guy said he passed the killer along the way. Which is why I'm so wet. I could see Trest's studio windows from where I stood."

"And I guess it's convenient that everyone knows not to disturb him while he's painting," I said.

"We'll get a warrant in the morning for the gallery and his studio," Jack said. "Maybe we'll find traces of blood or the rest of his clothing."

"Did you call Brian Dunnegan?" I asked.

Jack grabbed a bottle of water and I picked up my tea, and then we headed back toward the office.

"Oh, I called him," Jack said. "I told him about the baby, and he admitted that it was possible he was the father. But he has no intention of finding out for sure. Not even a flicker of emotion. He said he'd contact you in the morning. He doesn't want to go to the hassle of having her body transferred somewhere else. He said he'll have her cremated and if some of her friends want to give a memorial they're more than welcome to her. He said she was worth about as much to him as a pile of ashes as she was in real life."

"Ouch," I said. "What a horrible man."

"Speaking of," Jack said. "Did you happen to run any of the men on the list Rick Early gave us?"

"Not yet," I said. "I started the board, but I got sidetracked." I ran my finger along the computer pad, and the images came back on the whiteboard.

"Ahh," Jack said, taking a closer look at the crime scene photos from the original Jack the Ripper murders.

"I fell down the rabbit hole," I said.

"It's a good trail to go down."

We worked in silence for the next while, adding pictures of Brian Dunnegan and Peter Trest, and going about the painstaking task of adding the people who'd already been interviewed to the board as well.

"Four men on the list Rick Early gave us," Jack said. "Not including Trest. We can start running preliminary background checks on them. I wonder who the one right before Trest was? We can look at him first."

I glanced at the clock and noticed it was after ten. Doug hadn't called or texted, and I was hoping he made it home by curfew. I knew it was impor-tant to establish some boundaries. There had to be for this to work. And I really wanted it to work. It was the best thing for Doug.

"He'll be fine," Jack said. "He's still got time."

"I know, but it's been raining hard and steady. The roads might be flooded."

"All he's got to do is call."

Jack's cell phone rang as if it had needed permission first.

"See?" Jack held the phone up so I could see Doug's name on the screen. "Doug," he said. "Everything okay?"

Jack was an excellent poker player, but even I could tell something was wrong and it was confirmed when he said, "We'll be right there."

He hung up and I was already moving toward the mudroom. He followed behind me.

"Bring your bag," Jack said. "There was a shooting at the theater and two people are dead."

CHAPTER SEVEN

Only years of training kept me moving, my brain processing critical information while I gathered the supplies I needed.

"Is Doug hurt?" I asked.

"Just shaken up," Jack said. "He witnessed the whole thing. Smith is there with him and the girl."

Stewart Smith was one of Jack's sergeants, and he was a genuinely good guy. His mother owned Martha's Diner, and he came from a long line of cops. His dad had gone down in the line of duty, and Martha had been left to raise their seven boys on her own. She'd done a good job of it. Half of them were first responders and the rest were law-abiding citizens.

"Good," I said. I knew Smith would keep them safe and separated. He had kids of his own.

It was going to be cold and wet. There was no getting around it. But it was the victims I was worried about.

"See if whoever is on scene makes sure the victims stay dry," I said, opening the cabinet and pulling out my thick coveralls. They were the easiest thing to squat and maneuver in since a big coat got in the way. I topped the coveralls with a thin rain slicker, put on thick socks and rain boots, and pulled a toboggan down low over my ears.

Jack had stepped out of the room to make the call and I could hear his voice in the background but I wasn't paying attention to what he was saying. There was a knot in the center of my chest—a heaviness that made it hard to draw in a deep breath. I knew sound was happening around me, but all I could feel was pressure in my ears and the rush of blood.

I'd been in some of the most high-pressure situations imaginable. I'd worked relentless hours in the ER on little to no sleep, and I'd done what I'd been trained to do when life and death hung in the balance. Never had I wavered or faltered. I just did my job because it's what needed to be done.

Even when coming face to face with a killer or my father, I'd always been steady. I hadn't always been strong enough to fight back, but I'd been steady, even accepting as death had loomed over me.

But something was unraveling inside of me. The last time I'd had an anxiety attack was when I'd finally come back home to Bloody Mary. When I'd almost died at the hands of Jeremy Mooney, I'd tucked my tail between my legs and run. I'd resigned as coroner and closed the funeral home. But I'd known I couldn't stay gone forever, and I'd crept back in the middle of the night with that pressure on my chest and the memory of those fingers wrapped around my throat, cutting off the air.

I dropped back onto the built-in bench and put a hand to my chest. I tried to take in deep breaths, but the pressure in my chest wouldn't allow it. My skin went hot and then just as quickly went cool and clammy. Was I going into shock? Was I having a stroke? Why now?

I closed my eyes and tried to relax. I didn't want Jack to find me like this. There was too much at stake for him to be worrying about whether or not I could do the job. And I sure didn't want him trying to take on more of the load himself.

The clanging in my ears stopped and I could hear Jack still talking on the phone. This time I focused on his voice, on the words he was saying, and I felt my pulse start to slow. The breaths I was struggling to take started to come easier, and I opened my eyes and felt the world come back into focus. My palms were sweaty and my breathing was still rapid, but I could—and would—function.

I'd just gotten to my feet and was taking my bag off the hook when Jack came back in. He narrowed his eyes at me and asked, "What's wrong?"

"Nothing," I lied. "I'm just worried about Doug."

"You're white as a sheet," he said.

"I'm fine," I insisted.

Jack studied me for a few more seconds, and I thought he was going to press the issue, but thankfully, he let it go.

"I just got off the phone with Smith," Jack said. "He called for a makeshift tent to be set up over the victims. It's coming down pretty hard out there. The initial 911 call was made about fifteen minutes ago. Smith arrived within a couple of minutes, checked the victims to see if there was a pulse, and when he found none, he called in for backup and started work on securing the scene. He said EMTs arrived about five minutes later and confirmed death. They're sticking around to see if any witnesses need medical attention."

We went out the side door, and Jack set the alarm, securing the door behind us. Then he took my keys to the Suburban. There was no point in taking two vehicles, and I was glad he was driving. We had a garage with some of Jack's toys, and a car he'd bought for me, but somehow our work vehicles always ended up parked under the portico that connected the house and the garage, and the cars in the garage mostly went unused.

"Gang related?" I asked once we'd gotten in the Suburban.

"I don't know. The theater wasn't crowded, but Doug and a few other kids were hanging out under the marquee. Smith said a yellow car pulled up and opened fire, and then he sped off. There's an APB out on the car, but nothing so far."

"You need to call Carver," I said. "Doug's mom will want to know."

Jack sighed. "Yeah, you're right."

I adjusted the heat so it was blowing right on me, and tucked into the seat with my arms crossed over my chest. I was cold, and was having a hard time getting warm. Jack had his earbuds in, so I couldn't hear the other side of the conversation, but Jack laid out the facts and told Carver he'd keep him updated every step of the way.

The wipers swished rapidly and I could see the rising water in the ditches along Heresy Road. Jack hung up with Carver and then immediately got on the phone again, calling the station to make sure anyone who was on duty was out driving the roads to check for flooding. The last thing we wanted was to deal with citizens out driving around and ending up drowning on top of everything else that was going on.

There was only one movie theater in the county and it was in King George Proper, not far from the university. It was a good half-hour drive with the rain slowing us down, and I was worried about the wet and dropping temperature and how it would affect the victims. The good news was we had a pretty exact time of death. The other good news for me was that cases like this were pretty straightforward. I'd recover the ballistics during the autopsy and let the police do their jobs.

Old Towne Cinema had opened after I'd graduated from college, so I'd never been much of a patron. And now that Jack and I spent most of our time in the community with our work, when we did go to movies, we made sure to leave the county.

Old Towne housed twelve theaters in a concrete block of a building, but the front had a huge old-school marquee outlined in red and there was a clock tower reminiscent of the one in *Back to the Future* above it. The parking lot wasn't well lit and the trash can out front overflowed with soggy popcorn buckets and oversized soda cups. I noticed the news van parked just outside the perimeter that had been set up, and the crew was out in matching blue rainsuits and setting up a portable awning to protect the cameras.

I wasn't too worried about them. The crime scene wasn't visible from our side of the crime scene tape. Smith had done a good job setting up the tent over the bodies so curious onlookers couldn't see and the victims were protected.

Jack parked behind a couple of patrol cars. I lifted the hood of my rain jacket and tied it tight under my chin, and I went ahead and put on latex gloves over my leather gloves to keep from ruining them.

"Time to get wet," I said, and put the strap of my bag crossways over my body.

I'd been scanning the area and I hadn't seen Doug yet, but I knew Smith probably had him and any other witnesses back inside the theater and out of the cold.

The tent was nothing more than a couple of

poles and a blue tarp, but it had done the job and the victims lay mostly dry. A couple of high-powered lights had been set up and shone directly on the victims. It was a perfect still shot that told a story right up until the moment their lives had been taken.

"They're just kids," I said, looking at the round-ness of youth in their faces. A red umbrella lay upside down a couple of feet away from the boy. A small yellow purse had fallen next to the girl.

Jack stood next to me with his hands on his hips, looking down at a future that would never have a chance to blossom.

The boy had dark hair that clung to his damp face. He had Asian features, and he was tall and lanky, his jacket and shoes high quality.

I took some pictures of the scene from over-head. Jack squatted down beside him and checked his pockets for identification, and he pulled a wallet from inside his jacket pocket.

"Mark Lee," Jack said, holding a driver's license up to the light. "Age nineteen."

I took an evidence bag and held it open so he could drop the wallet inside, and then I waited while Jack checked the rest of his pockets. There were car keys, a ticket stub, and a pack of gum, but not much else to tell us the story of Mark Lee.

"Seven o'clock showing," Jack said, looking at the ticket stub. "They must have just been coming out from seeing the movie."

Jack moved around to the other side and picked

up the small purse, looking for the girl's identi-fication.

"Tatiana Russo," Jack said. "Age seventeen." He put her purse in another evidence bag and then checked her coat pockets, but there was nothing in them. "We'll send the grief counselor and the police chaplain to her address to talk with her parents since she's still a minor."

"It's okay if you need to go check on Doug," I told him, kneeling down next to the boy.

"Doug's okay," Jack said. "He's texted a couple of times and said that Sergeant Smith is pretty funny. We'll go in and see him together once you're done here. They deserve to not lie here any longer than they have to."

I nodded, knowing he was right. Our first priority had to be to the victim. We were all they had.

The bullet had caught the boy square in the chest. I unzipped his jacket and parted it, exposing his blood-soaked hoodie.

"Center mass," I said. I used my finger to probe around the entry wound and then took the small ruler from my bag and measured the size of the hole. "About half an inch. I don't see any other trauma to the front of the body. No other GSWs. Let's turn him and see if it exited."

Jack helped me turn Mark Lee to his side and I whistled. "I guess it exited." A softball-size hole had bloomed open in his back from where the bullet had found a way out.

"You're looking at a .44 or maybe a .357," Jack said. "That's the kind of gun meant to kill if you pull the trigger."

"But where did it go?" I asked, rolling Mark back to the ground.

Jack and I both got to our feet, and he took his high-beam flashlight out of his pocket. I looked at the positioning of the bodies and the entry wounds and then I walked toward the ticket booth.

Jack shone his light against the concrete wall between the ticket booth and the exit doors, and about three feet from the ground was the bullet embedded in the wall.

"There's one of them," Jack said.

I handed him a pair of tweezers and a smaller evidence bag, and I took the flashlight. He called one of the officers standing guard and asked for a yellow evidence marker to put in place and then he carefully removed the bullet from the wall.

I recognized the officer—his last name was Derby, though I wasn't sure I'd ever heard his first name—but we'd never worked a case together before. I didn't have a lot of interaction with the guys that worked nights.

"Any casings found?" Jack asked.

"No, sir," Derby said. "Smith and a couple of us checked as we walked off the perimeter."

"There are cameras," I said, pointing to the black globes on the ceiling. "Maybe between these and the parking lot cameras we can get an identity."

Jack nodded and then stuck the bag in his jacket pocket. "Who else is on scene?"

"Well, Nash was on call, but he said he's stuck on Moor Gate Road. There's a tree down and he can't get across. Otherwise it's just me, Sarge, and Walters."

"Y'all did good," Jack said. "The scene is tight. Now we just have to find the other bullet. Why don't you and Walters track down the manager and start looking through camera footage. If we can get a good facial clip we can get it out for the early morning news. Maybe someone will recognize him."

"Yes, Sir," Derby said and whistled at Walters for him to go with him.

"Found it," I said, shining the flashlight onto the pavement. "This one fragmented."

Jack used the tweezers and collected what he could find of the fragments, and then he placed another marker for the crime scene techs.

"I'm going to look at the female," I told Jack, and headed back under the tent.

Her small frame hadn't stood a chance against a .44. The entry wound was in the upper shoulder, and she was a good bit shorter than her date. Which was why her bullet trajectory had ended up in the pavement. Mark had most likely died instantly, but she had probably lingered a couple of minutes before she bled out.

It didn't take me long to come to the same conclusion on her as I had for Mark—no other wounds, no other trauma. Cause of death was a single gunshot wound. I'd have to do an autopsy to make it formal, but it was just to dot the i's and cross the t's.

Jack came back over just as I was finishing up. "Anything else?" he asked.

"Nope, we can move them to the lab," I said. "We're going to need some transport help."

"EMTs are still here," he said. "Let's get them bagged and loaded and then go see Doug. I want to find out what happened here."

CHAPTER EIGHT

THE EMTs HELPED US BAG AND LOAD THE VICTIMS on the two ambulances at the scene, and Jack and I were finally free to find Doug. It hadn't been long since we'd gotten the initial call, but it seemed like an eternity.

"Derby," Jack said, once we were inside. "Any luck on the cams?"

"Yeah, they've got a full system in place—interior, exterior, and parking lot. We've got the make and model of the vehicle, but we're hoping maybe IT can clean up the visual of the perp. Between the rain and the camera quality it's not the best shot."

"I've got someone who can work on it tonight," Jack said. "Any trouble with the manager and getting copies?

"No, sir," Derby said. "He's been very cooperative. Walters is getting the copies now."

"Where have they stashed the witnesses?" Jack asked.

"Theater one," Derby said, pointing to a door across the lobby. "Sarge has everyone in there, and he's been taking statements. Should almost be done."

"Thanks, Derby," Jack said. "Good work tonight."

"Yeah, well, I hope we catch the bastard," Derby said. "Kids should be able to go to the movies without having to worry about stuff like this. Especially in King George."

That was the thing about evil—it permeated and crept its way into the cracks and crevices that had been left vacant or no one paid attention to it any longer. The naïvety of people never ceased to amaze me. They believed in things like peace on earth and that evil would cease to exist if we just loved more.

But evil had belonged to the earth since Adam and Eve fell, and it would flourish as long as there was the thirst for hatred and war and power and greed. Evil is like the serpent—cunning and deceptive—it lies dormant...until one day it doesn't. And then everyone is surprised because they don't know how another person could do something like that. But that root of sin is in all of us—though what we do with it is our choice. Some people choose poorly. And people like Mark Lee and Tatiana Russo pay the price.

The theater was small. The walls and carpets were dark purple, and there were red and pink flowers on the carpet that reminded me of something from *Little Shop of Horrors*. I scanned the room and counted a dozen people—couples huddled together closely and friends weeping silently. Smith seated down front taking a statement from the blonde girl who'd picked up Doug from our house.

Then there was Doug, leaning against the wall. He saw us and the relief on his face was obvious.

"Boy, am I glad to see you guys," he said, rushing toward us.

I thought he was going to give me a hug, but he seemed to change his mind at the last minute, as if he wasn't sure that was something he was supposed to do. I solved the problem for him and pulled him into a hug.

"Are you okay?" I asked, squeezing him tighter than was probably comfortable.

"I'm okay," he said.

I looked at his face closely, but his eyes were steady and clear. Doug wanted to be a cop, and he'd worked as a consultant on some cases with us before. He'd seen more than the normal teenager, but I wanted to make sure he didn't become so hardened to scenes like what happened outside that he forgot there were real people and emotions involved.

"Really," he assured me, and I nodded and backed away so Jack could give his own hug.

"I mean, I was totally freaked out when it happened," Doug said, looking pleased at the affection from Jack. "I've been in some close calls, but

I've never been shot at. It just happened so fast. Man, I'm starving. We've been stuck in here forever and they shut down the snack bar."

"It's been an hour since the 911 call came through," Jack said.

"Well, it feels like forever," Doug said, giving a lopsided smile that was very like his uncle's. He looked enough like Carver to be his son instead of his nephew, with the same blond hair and puppy dog eyes.

"We'll get you fed," Jack said. "Can you walk us through it?"

"Sure," Doug said. "I already told Sarge what I saw. He's talking with Tamara right now. She's my date. I really was going to be home by curfew. I swear."

I nodded and said, "I know you were. None of this is your fault."

"Yeah, well, it feels like it is," he said. "I opened the door for that couple. The ones that got shot. I opened the door and they went out first, and then Tamara's shoe got gum on the bottom of it and we kind of moved out of the way so she could scrape it off.

"We were all just kind of standing around under the marquee. It was raining pretty hard and no one wanted to run out to the parking lot. But the guy, the one that got shot, he had an umbrella and I guess they were going to make a run for it because they went out to the curb. And then this yellow car comes barreling through the parking lot, and in my head I'm thinking the guy is an idiot and he's going to hit someone cause he's going so fast.

"And I guess the guy with the umbrella and his date thought so too, because they just stopped and waited for him to pass by. But the yellow car slammed on the brakes right in front of them. Then the window rolled down and he shot them. Just like that. No warning or nothing. Everyone started screaming and the car drove away. I couldn't see the license plate through the rain."

"We were able to get it from the cameras," Jack said.

"Oh, good," Doug said, as if a weight had been lifted off his shoulders. "Anyway, Tamara called 911, and me and that lady over there..." He stopped and pointed at a middle-aged woman in jeans and a sweatshirt. Her face was set in hard lines and her eyes were scanning the crowd, and her blond-streaked hair had frizzed around her face as it had dried. She reminded me of a cop.

"She said she's a nurse," Doug said. "So we ran over to see if we could help them." Doug swallowed and his face lost some of its color. "I could tell the guy was dead right off. He turned kind of gray, and his eyes were closed, but I checked for a pulse.

"The nurse went to work right away on the girl. She was still alive, and you could see she was scared. I just talked to her while the nurse put pressure on her shoulder to try and stop the bleeding, but there wasn't anything she could do. She went fast."

It was then I noticed the streaks of dried blood on Doug's hoodie.

"You did the right thing," Jack assured him.

Doug blew out a shaky breath and he looked away uncomfortably. "We didn't have to wait on the police for very long. Sarge showed up just a couple of minutes later."

"What can you tell me about the shooter?" Jack asked.

"He was driving a yellow Ford Fusion," Doug said automatically. "Looked pretty new. Had temp tags, but like I said, I couldn't read them."

"Could you see the shooter?" Jack asked.

"Light skin," Doug said, his brow furrowed. "Kind of curly dark hair and weird sideburns. Round face. Had on big black sunglasses. He just looked like a guy. Nothing remarkable about him."

"What hand did he shoot from?" Jack asked.

"I don't know," Doug said, his frustration obvious. "I didn't see a gun. I just heard the shots and then those people dropped to the ground. It could have been any of us. It was just so fast."

Jack put his hand on Doug's shoulder and squeezed. "I know. You did good. Did Smith already take your statement?"

"Yeah, I was first since he knew who I was. How long before we can go home?"

"We just need to wrap up a few things and then we're gone," Jack said. "Call your uncle."

Sleep wasn't on my agenda. My body was exhausted, but my brain hadn't gotten the memo yet. The EMTs followed us to the funeral home, and we got the two newest residents settled in the cooler so I could start work on them tomorrow. Then we headed home.

I'd grown up in Bloody Mary and knew the roads and houses like the back of my hand. It wasn't a town of new construction, where different neighborhoods popped up every time you blinked, but the houses had character and had been renovated time and time again as they'd passed hands to new owners.

There were police cruisers with flashing lights at the end of Anne Boleyn as we made our way toward home. Water covered the streets in areas, and I could see blockades where it was no longer safe for cars to travel.

"It's been a long time since we've seen rain like this," I said. "I'm wondering if I should've stayed the night at the funeral home. We might not be able to make it back into town come morning."

"Umm...I'm going to pass on that," Doug said, sticking his head between our seats like a dog. "I mean, maybe it would be cool if I could invite a bunch of friends and we could do a kind of haunted house and freak ourselves out knowing we're in the same house as dead people. Maybe you could set that up for Halloween or something. But I'm already kind of at my limit because of what happened tonight, so I don't think I can add more freak-out on top of that without serious conse-quences. And all my equipment is at the house, and I kind of just want to zone out and play *Dragon Wars*. I could do with some hot chocolate too."

Sometimes it was hard to remember Doug was only sixteen.

"We're all sleeping at home," Jack assured him. "One of the deputies checked out our street and said we're good. Our elevation is a little higher so most of the rainwater is draining down toward the valley straight into town. The creeks and the rivers are already at capacity and waters are still rising, so there might be some people who wake up to wet floors in the morning. We've sent out a flooding alert and told people to stay off the streets, but that only goes so far once the workday starts. And I'm sure we have hot chocolate somewhere, unless you already drank it all."

"Nah, I have to be presented with the right opportunity for hot chocolate," Doug said. "And this seems like the right opportunity."

"I've got copies of the security cameras from the theater if you want to look at them for us," Jack said casually. "They're not the best pictures and the rain distorted things some. We'd like to try and get a clear picture of the shooter to put out to the media."

"Sure, I can take a look," Doug said. "I'll even waive my standard fee since I'm directly involved."

"I thought your standard fee was a rent-free

place to live and a bottomless pantry," I said, looking back at Doug.

He just grinned and said, "It never hurts to try. Besides, Uncle Ben told me you're putting all my consulting fees in a savings account so I don't blow it on video games and robot parts."

"Mostly because of the robot parts," I said.

"I don't know where your fear of robots comes from," he said. "I bet I could get every electronic thing in your kitchen to communicate with each other and do the work too. How awesome would it be to have breakfast waiting for you when you come down in the mornings?"

"That's what I got married for," I said, making Jack snicker. "And with Jack, I don't have to worry about him short-circuiting and beating me to death with a frying pan."

"Hey, humans have faulty wiring too," Doug said.

"Not Jack," I assured him. "But we'll talk again if he ever starts acting strange."

By the time Jack hit the remote for our gate, we were more than ready to be out of the car.

"We should get a dog," Doug said. "You've got all this space and a fenced-in yard. Wouldn't it be nice to have someone to come home to?"

"We've got you," Jack said, grinning at Doug in the rearview. "You even run to the door when we walk in and ask for a treat."

"Very funny," Doug said dryly.

But I looked at Jack out of the corner of my eye.

The seed had been planted, and I knew we'd end up with a dog sooner or later. Jack felt very strongly that kids Doug's age should have the responsibility of a pet. I'd never had any pets. I couldn't even keep my plants alive.

Jack pulled under the portico, and we filed out, going in the side door through the mudroom. I hung my rain gear on the rack and said to Doug, "Hand over your sweatshirt and I'll put it in the washer. I've got industrial-strength stuff that'll take the stains out."

Doug looked taken aback for a minute, as if he wasn't sure he wanted to keep the sweatshirt, but he pulled it off and handed it to me. And then he ran after Jack to the kitchen.

I went to the second floor where the laundry room was and stripped out of the jumpsuit, treating the stains before dumping it all in the washing machine and turning it on. I decided while I was upstairs to go up one more floor to our bedroom and change into something comfortable. I found soft gray sweats and slippers and then moved to the bathroom to wash my face. If I stayed busy—kept in motion—I wouldn't think about how close we'd come to losing Doug.

The water was cold as it filled my hands, and I watched, mesmerized by the endless overflow as droplets trickled down the blue veins in my arms. I didn't look at myself in the mirror. I knew I'd see a wild-eyed reflection there, and I didn't want to think about the anxiety attack I'd had before we left the scene for fear that it would return.

I'd always longed for family. I'd understood at a young age that the one I'd been born to was abnormal at best and horrifically dysfunctional at worst. I'd watched other children with envy, wondering what it must be like to have parents who actually loved you. I'd always thought there'd been something wrong with me—something that made me unlovable. I hadn't learned until a few years ago that I'd just been a cover—stolen from the womb of my biological mother—and brought back to make it look like we were an all-American family.

I'd had Jack and friends like Vaughn and Dickey and Eddie growing up, and I guess we'd made our own kind of family. But now that I had some distance to look back, there'd been no need for any of them to make a family with me. They'd had normal parents who loved them and did the things parents were supposed to do—which didn't include smuggling soldiers into their basement whose bodies had been filled with money and weapons. So it hadn't been them who'd needed family. It had just been me.

But I'd finally gotten the family I'd always longed for when I married Jack. And over the last couple of years our circle had expanded—Carver, Michelle, Lily, Sheldon, Emmy Lu, Cole, and now Doug. This was family.

Back when Jack had taken those bullets to the chest and his life had hung in the balance, I'd tried to imagine what life might be like without him. Even before we'd been a couple, I hadn't been able to fathom the idea of life without him in it. That had been the first time I realized what hero life looked like, and what it meant for the people who loved heroes.

It made me realize that the more family you had—the more people you loved—the more fragile the web that tangled it all together. I could see how easy it would be for evil to start cutting at those web strings. Because whether we liked it or not, once we decided to stand for good—for justice—there was no choice but to face the darkness head-on. And protecting what I loved most—my family —was more important than anything else.

I splashed the cold water on my face and dried it briskly with a towel, and then headed back downstairs with a new determination. The best way to keep my family safe was to keep doing what we'd always done. Hunting the bad guys and putting them away forever.

I smelled the hot chocolate before I got to the kitchen, and my stomach rumbled, reminding me we'd never eaten dinner.

"The oven is heating up," Jack said when I came in. "There were a couple of pizzas in the freezer."

He handed me a mug of hot chocolate piled high with marshmallows and studied my face carefully. "You okay?"

"I'm fine," I said.

"You keep saying that, but somehow I don't think it's true."

I gave him a half smile and popped a marshmallow into my mouth. "Let me put it this way," I said. "I'm better now. I'd like to finish what we can on the board tonight. Juliet Dunnegan's killer is still out there. There's not much we can do about what happened tonight until the car is located or until Doug is able to get a visual on the shooter."

"I'm on it," Doug said. "Right after I destroy this pizza."

"We'll find him," Jack said. "There can't be too many bright yellow cars driving around in a rainstorm."

"Tamara texted and said her parents are super freaked out," Doug said. "They want her to move out of her apartment and back home. She said they're just scared and overreacting, but I think they're going to call you tomorrow."

"That's fine," Jack said. "Feel free to give them my cell number. How did you meet Tamara?"

"She's part of my *Dragon Wars* league," Doug said, shrugging. "She's pretty cool."

"And how old is Tamara?" Jack asked.

"We haven't really talked about that," Doug said, avoiding eye contact, but his cheeks went scarlet. "She's doing her undergrad at KGU."

"And let me guess," Jack said. "You told her you're working on your master's degree."

"Well, I am," he said, tilting his chin defiantly.

"I know you are," Jack said. "But you're not telling the whole truth. You're a minor. And these girls are adults. The law goes both ways, and they need to know that you're only sixteen."

"You don't understand," Doug said. "Do you know how hard it is to be my age and everyone around you all the time is at least ten years older? Girls my age are in high school. That was forever ago."

"I do get it," Jack said. "But you can't go into any relationship, romantic or otherwise, by deceiving the other person. Look at it from the other way—if you were in your early twenties and you started dating a girl you thought was your age—only to discover she was sixteen. And then imagine what would happen if you added sex into mix. Things would get ugly really fast."

I hadn't realized Doug could get any redder, but somehow, he managed. He'd eaten all his marshmallows from the mug and went straight for the bag. "Yeah, I get it," he said. "But it still sucks."

"Just be you," Jack said. "And I'm not saying you can't go out and have fun with your friends. But truth matters. And having that kind of integrity at sixteen is going to shape the man you eventually become."

Doug blew on his hot chocolate and said, "Yeah, yeah. I *do* get it. I'll tell them the truth. I promise."

I slipped out of the kitchen, feeling like I'd been eavesdropping on a very guy conversation, and I headed to the office. I turned on the computer and pressed the button so my previous work showed back up on the whiteboard.

I added pictures of Brian Dunnegan and Peter Trest directly below the picture of Juliet. It seemed like a lifetime ago that we'd talked with either man, though it had been less than twenty-four hours. Neither of them had an alibi for the time when Juliet was murdered.

I didn't have a copy of the sketch Samson had made from the witness's description, so I'd have to wait for Jack on that. But I did have the names of the four men Rick Early had given us.

I typed each of their names into the computer to run a background check, and DMV records were the first things to appear. I put four driver's license pictures beneath the images of Brian and Peter.

Jeffrey Goldstein. Antonio Corelli. Cameron Blanchard. James Dupont.

All handsome men. Two of them married. Juliet didn't seem to mind where her lovers came from or if they were attached. According to Trest, her philosophy was to move on when she got bored. But not from her husband. Just from her lovers.

I made a note to call Rick Early in the morning and ask who her lover was just before Trest.

Jack came in carrying two plates that had a couple of slices of pizza on them in one hand, and two bottles of beer in the other.

"My hero," I said. "I'm starving."

"You sound like Doug."

"How is he?" I asked.

"He'll be all right," Jack said. "He's got a good head on his shoulders, and he wants to do the right thing. If more people wanted to do the right thing then we'd have a lot less work to do."

"Very true," I said, taking the plate from him and pushing over so we could both sit behind the desk. "Do you have Samson's sketch? I want to do a comparison."

Jack opened his laptop and logged in, and a couple of minutes later the sketch appeared on the whiteboard.

"Wow," I said. "That's underwhelming."

"I know," Jack said, taking a bite of pizza. "He could be anyone. Nondescript features."

He typed with one hand another set of commands and the security camera footage appeared next to the sketch.

"I'd guess the mustache is a fake," Jack said. "It's too memorable. The top hat is hiding the brow and eye line, and his hair is covering the top of the ears. He's probably wearing a wig too."

"We need to find a motive," I said.

"I'm going to start getting warrants in the morning," Jack said. "Between the baby and a divorce settlement, the men in her life have plenty of motive. It's just narrowing it down."

"I guess there's nothing more we can do here tonight," I said.

"We can get some sleep," Jack said. "Sometimes there's nothing you can do but wait for daylight."

"I'm not tired," I said, looking at my empty plate.

Jack pulled me from my chair and into his lap. "I can probably find something to help with that."

CHAPTER NINE

"I'M REALLY TIRED OF THE RAIN," I SAID, CRACKING open an eye and staring at the droplets sliding down the big picture windows in our bedroom. "Everything is damp. I wouldn't be surprised if the entire house just floated away down the Potomac."

"Feeling dramatic this morning?" Jack asked. He was snuggled in behind me and his arm was around my waist. It was rare he wasn't up before me.

"Maybe a little," I said. "I'm trying it out to see if it will stick."

"That's very theatrical of you."

"It's going around," I said, thinking of Juliet Dunnegan. "You being lazy this morning?"

"Maybe a little," he said, making me grin. "Someone kept me up past my bedtime last night."

"Sounds like you should be grateful," I said, laughing as his fingers found my ribs. "What time is it?"

"Much too late for what you're thinking," Jack said, nipping my ear playfully. "But I'll go start the coffee and then I'll meet you in the shower. Maybe we can multitask."

"I like multitasking," I said, tossing back the covers. "I've got a surprise for you."

"I like it when you're feeling dramatic," he said, jumping out of bed and pulling on a pair of sweatpants.

"Better hurry," I said, waggling my eyebrows and giving my hips a little extra twitch as I walked into the bathroom. "I might start without you."

"You've got a full day today," Jack said, standing over the frying pan. The smell of scrambled eggs and cheese permeated the air, and Jack expertly poured everything onto tortillas for breakfast burritos.

"Brian Dunnegan is going to have to come by and fill out the paperwork if he wants Juliet cremated," I said. "But yeah, between our victims last night and getting Juliet prepped, it's going to be a full day. And that's assuming I won't have any more visitors."

"I like how you call them visitors, as if they're dropping in for drinks and a conversation," Jack said, putting a plate in front of me.

"Well, technically they are visiting. They're not moving in. And sometimes we have really great conversations. It's like therapy. I get a lot off my chest, and they don't judge me in return. We don't have drinks though. That would be weird."

Jack snorted. "I think you've already crossed that bridge."

"Don't get sassy or I'll let Peter Trest paint me. He appreciates my bone structure."

"While I'm not arguing that your bone structure is, in fact, fantastic, I think Trest's appreciation has more to do with the fact that you're female and breathing. He's a hound dog."

I widened my eyes and then blinked rapidly. "Say it ain't so! I've never met one of those before."

He grinned and said, "Shut up. Besides, I'm a reformed hound dog. Completely domesticated."

"And housebroken," I said.

"You'd better go to work before you get in trouble," he said, narrowing his eyes.

I grinned unrepentantly and got up to put my empty plate in the sink. I smacked him on the behind on my way out of the kitchen, feeling like the day was off to a good start.

***

Emmy Lu was already at her desk by the time I'd navigated my way through the streets that had turned to rivers overnight. And since the people of Bloody Mary were contrary on their best days, they'd all decided to get in their cars and drive around to see how bad the flooding was. Which meant cops and firefighters were spending their morning rerouting traffic and pulling people out of high-water situations.

Emmy Lu's things were hung neatly in the mudroom—a bright pink raincoat and matching boots with little red cherries on them. And then I took a closer look at her boots and realized they were steel toed. If an outfit could perfectly sum up a person, it was this one. Emmy Lu looked like a middle-aged soccer mom who specialized in baking cookies and knitting sweaters, but she could stab a person in the eye with her knitting needles and never blink. She was tough, and her five boys could attest to that.

I could hear her moving around the kitchen and smell the coffee brewing.

"You must have gotten here at the crack of dawn," I said, adjusting my sweater. I'd dressed for business today in black leggings and a bright red cowl-neck sweater that came down to mid-thigh. I sat down on the barstool at the island and put on my black knee-high boots.

"About half an hour ago," she said, putting creamer and sugar in the center of the island and then filling two mugs with coffee.

"How were the roads from your place?" I asked. "I wondered if you'd even be able to come in today." Emmy Lu lived in what we affectionately called the "boondocks" and her one-lane gravel road tended to wash out in bad weather.

"Oh, they're flooded," she said. "But the house is fine. Two of the boys are holding down the fort."

The confusion on my face must have been obvious because Emmy Lu's cheeks went pink. "Tom's house is closer. He offered to let me stay so I could make it in to work today."

I arched a brow at that. "I bet he did," I said, disguising a smile by blowing on my coffee.

Tom Daly owned the donut shop on the square, and he and Emmy Lu had been sharing more than donut recipes.

"Stop that," she said, waving her hand scoldingly in my direction. "Tom's a gentleman."

"You've got a bite mark on your neck," I told her, and she slapped a hand over the side of her neck and went to look at her reflection in the toaster.

"Well," Emmy Lu said, returning to the island and her coffee. "Gentlemen can be animals too."

I burst out laughing. "And he gave you donuts too. I can smell them."

She shook her head. "You've got a gift." She opened the oven and pulled out two boxes of donuts from where she'd been keeping them warm.

"It's my superpower," I said. "I can always sniff out hot buttery sugar, no matter where you put it. I put the paperwork for Juliet Dunnegan on your desk."

"I saw it," she said, taking a bite of donut. "It's a sad situation. Tom took me to see that play she was in early last week. We dressed up and everything. I recognized her picture from the program."

"Notice anything weird?" I asked.

"What could be weird about a room full of adults dressed up like a bunch of Charles Dickens rejects? We only went because they gave away free mulled cider with every ticket purchase. I needed the buzz at intermission. Tom just slept through the whole thing."

"Her husband is supposed to come by later and sign paperwork. He wants her cremated as quickly as possible."

"No viewing?" Emmy Lu asked.

"Her head was detached," I told her. "It's not an open casket situation."

Emmy Lu winced.

"Besides, he doesn't seem too keen on drawing out the mourning period. I wouldn't be surprised if he dumped her ashes in the garbage on the way out. There's no love lost between him and Juliet."

"That's a shame," Emmy Lu said, shaking her head. "It seems like you should mourn the person you swore to love until death do you part."

The mudroom door flew open with a crash, and Emmy Lu and I both leaned back to see what had happened.

"Sorry about that," Lily called out. "The wind caught the door. It's a mess out there. I smell donuts."

"Lily has a superpower too," I said.

"What superpower?" Sheldon asked, peeking around Lily. He was wearing down coveralls in camo brown and a matching jacket, and he was dripping all over the floor. Everything looked two times too big for him.

"Twelve percent of people in this country believe they have a legitimate superpower," Sheldon said.

"What counts as legitimate?" Emmy Lu asked.

Lily hung up her red raincoat and umbrella and helped Sheldon get the coat unzipped because he couldn't reach the zipper down around his knees.

"Things like psychic powers or telekinesis," he said. "Or those people on the infomercials who can always predict who the next president is going to be."

The more layers Sheldon pulled off, the higher my eyebrows rose. He was stuffed into a pair of black western dress pants rolled up at the hem and a pair of snakeskin boots. He wore the same black-and-yellow checkered shirt he'd worn yesterday, though I was guessing it had been washed since it was freshly ironed. He wore a black belt with a big silver buckle that actually fit.

"Wow," Emmy Lu said. "Don't you look snazzy. You going two-stepping after work?"

"I don't know," Sheldon said. "Should I? I don't know how to two-step."

"I'll teach you," Emmy Lu said.

"We got stranded at Cole's place last night," Lily said, moving to the coffeepot. She was dressed in fresh clothes—tan suede leggings and a creamy white loose blouse that she made look fashionable with a wide leather belt that matched her boots.

She looked very put together for someone who got caught at Cole's house because of the storm.

"So have you moved in yet?" Emmy Lu asked, obviously coming to the same conclusion. "You've obviously brought over more than a toothbrush."

"We've got drawer space," Lily said. "And some closet space. It's more convenient, especially since his hours are erratic. Did you run into something with your neck? Maybe some teeth?"

Sheldon polished his glasses and then put them back on, eyeing Emmy Lu's neck closely. "How do you run into teeth?" he asked.

"It's a quandary," Emmy Lu said, tugging up the collar of her shirt and narrowing her eyes at Lily. Lily just smiled and took a donut.

"How's Doug?" Lily asked. "Cole told me about what happened last night."

"What happened?" Emmy Lu asked. "I'm not shacked up with a cop so I'm behind on all the tea. How about you pour a hot cup?"

"What does tea have to do with shacking up with a cop?" Sheldon asked. "I'm not shacked up with a cop. Maybe I should be though. They do seem to be well informed."

"Tea means gossip," Lily told him. "It's slang. And stay away from cops. They're hard on relationships."

Emmy Lu and I both zeroed in on Lily, and Sheldon said, "There's irony in your warning. You're in a relationship with a cop." The confusion on his face was real.

Lily smiled sweetly and said, "That's because I like a challenge, and I've got a hard head. A lady cop would tear you up and spit you out. We'll go meet Annie today at the shipping store. Trust me on this."

"Hello," Emmy Lu said dramatically. "This is me standing here with no tea. Would someone please tell me what happened to Doug?"

"Drive-by shooting at Old Towne," I told her.

She gasped and put her hand to her chest. "Ohmigosh."

"He's okay," I assured her. "Doug and his date and a few other people were standing under the marquee after the movie and this car pulls up and opens fire. Then they sped off."

Emmy Lu shook her head in disbelief. "This world is going to hell in a handbasket. Have they caught him?"

"Not that I know of," I said. "Both victims died at the scene. I've got them in the cooler downstairs, so that's what my morning looks like."

"You've got an incoming from the hospital too," Emmy Lu said. "Louise Chalmers. Eighty years old. Natural causes. Family asked for her to be transported in. I've got a call in to set up an appointment and see to the funeral details, but I don't have an idea for when the body will arrive. Things are kind of backlogged with the weather."

"Okay," I said. "Sheldon can handle her when she comes in. I need to get started on the autopsies and get everything back to Jack."

"I've got some reading to do in between work," Lily said. "I've got a body farm weekend coming up, so I'll fly out Thursday night and be back at work Tuesday morning."

"You're good for a little while," I told her. "You can use my office if you want. I'll let you know if we get busy. People tend to die on days like this when it's most inconvenient."

"At least it's not a full moon," Emmy Lu said.

"Did you know in the Middle Ages scientists thought full moons triggered seizures and other psychotic episodes?" Sheldon asked. He eyed the last donut and then snatched it quickly before he could change his mind. "That's where the term lunatics came from. It means moon sick."

"Fascinating," Emmy Lu said. "Let's hope the lunatics stay home today."

CHAPTER TEN

I LEFT THE OTHERS WITH THEIR COFFEE AND DONUTS and headed down to the lab to get started on the autopsies. Before I rolled the first body from the cooler, I stopped to look up the number for the theater in Newcastle.

"Rick Early, please," I said when a woman answered the phone.

I waited less than a minute before his voice came on the line. "This is Rick."

"This is Dr. Graves with the coroner's office," I said. "We spoke yesterday."

"Of course," he said. "Have you found out anything new?"

"We're still investigating," I said. "Do you happen to know who Juliet dated right before Peter Trest?"

"Oh, sure," he said. "That was Bruno Corelli."

"For real?" I asked, making Rick chuckle. "There's no Bruno on the list you gave me."

"Antonio," he said. "I think Bruno is his middle name. That's what he goes by. And his and Juliet's relationship didn't last long. Bruno's a hothead and he's the jealous type. I think Juliet put up with it a couple of weeks before she dropped him. He kept pushing for her to leave her husband, and she always made it very clear she had no intention of doing that."

"Did she leave Bruno for Trest?" I asked.

"I don't think so," Rick said. "If I recall, if was actually a while before anyone found out about Trest. He doesn't make it a habit of dating local women. He's kind of high profile. But someone saw her coming out of his studio in the middle of the night, so the cat was kind of out of the bag at that point."

"I guess so," I said. Someone was trying to call and I took the phone away from my ear long enough to see it was Jack. "Thanks for your help, Rick. I've got another call I've got to take."

"Any time," he said, and I answered Jack's call before it went to voicemail.

"Are you wrist deep in autopsies?" he asked. "I was hoping to catch you before you started."

"I've been at work an hour," I said. "Why would you assume I hadn't started yet?"

"Cause I ran into Tom Daly this morning and he mentioned that he gave Emmy Lu a couple of dozen donuts to bring to work."

"That dirty snitch," I said, mouth dropping

open. "Did he mention that Emmy Lu stayed the night with him?"

Jack laughed. "No, he didn't mention that. I just wanted to call and tell you we found the car."

"From last night?" I asked, dropping into my desk chair. "What about the shooter?"

"We found the car out on Cromwell Street. It washed out and was blocking traffic. No sign of the driver, but we did find the gun inside the glove box."

"Cromwell is in the middle of nowhere," I said. "Where would he have gone in this kind of weather at that time of night?"

"We found some pretty deep tracks in the mud," Jack said. "Must have been a truck or something with a pretty sizeable weight. The rain would've covered up regular tire tracks, but we could still see these. Won't be able to get anything but photographs though until things dry out some."

"So he picked the yellow car for a reason," I said. "Curious why he'd pick something so visible."

"And then we have to wonder if that was the plan all along or if he was improvising because of the weather. Cromwell is definitely the road less traveled. And it's probably a fifteen-minute drive from the theater. Risky considering how fast we got the APB issued."

"He knows the area," I said. "Knew how to navigate where he was going in the dark and in the rain. Had a getaway vehicle waiting and ditched the yellow car, and then drove home. Cromwell is right on the line between Nottingham and Newcastle. Or maybe he had an accomplice who picked him up."

"We're impounding the vehicle and we'll see if we can pull any prints or find anything that might point us in the right direction. We're running a DMV search right now to see who it's registered to."

"I talked to Rick Early a few minutes ago," I said. "A guy by the name of Bruno Corelli was Juliet's lover before Peter Trest."

"Bruno Corelli?" Jack asked. "Seriously?"

"Rick said it's his middle name."

"I'll see what I can find out," Jack said. "I'm waiting for warrants, and we're neck deep in 911 calls because everyone listens so well. Let me know when you're finished with the autopsies and we'll go pay a visit to Bruno."

"Sounds like a plan," I said. "Love you."

"Love you too."

I checked the time and knew I had at least four to five hours of autopsy work in front of me, so there was no point in delaying the inevitable. I turned on Nat King Cole and got to work.

I rolled Tatiana Russo back into the cooler, feeling mildly disappointed. Autopsies made sense to me. They were a piece to an always bigger puzzle. The body often gave witness testimony as well as any living person—sometimes even better.

But Tatiana and Mark had died senselessly.

There had been no revelation. No hidden clues. Each had suffered a single gunshot for no rhyme or reason. Jack would look into the friends and families, see if they had any gang or drug associations. But there'd been no drugs in their system. No markings or tattoos on their bodies to say they belonged to any organization. They'd just been teenagers, getting a handle on life. Maybe a little bit in love. I didn't have anything to give to Jack that would help him with this case.

I cleaned up and shut everything down, anxious to get out of the basement and get some fresh air. I knew Emmy Lu had control of the funeral home, though I did wonder why we hadn't received Louise Chalmers yet. I'd fully expected for Sheldon to come down to start the embalming process while I'd been working.

There was no one in the kitchen, and I checked my office, but Lily wasn't there. I had a text from Jack letting me know he was free whenever I was ready. The rain was still coming down, but it was lighter than it had been. I switched out my boots and put on my coat, hat, and scarf, and then locked the side door behind me.

I breathed in the frigid air, letting it expand in my lungs. It felt good. I dug in my pocket and pulled out my gloves, and then made my way down the ramp to the Suburban. I wished I had one of those cars that started and heated up by remote, but it seemed frivolous to get rid of a perfectly good transport vehicle just for the luxury of heating up my seats from inside the house.

Catherine of Aragon was higher in the middle of the road so drainage ran off to both sides, but as I backed out of the driveway I realized the water couldn't drain if there was no place else for it to go.

So I drove in the middle of the road toward the Town Square. I was glad to see there weren't as many people on the roads, and several of the businesses I passed were closed down, but whatever hissy fit Mother Nature was having was wreaking havoc on the county. I couldn't remember the last time we'd had flooding like this. Maybe not ever.

The sheriff's office had recently taken over the entire municipal building once the new fire station was built, and renovations had been slow going through the holiday season and the rain. They were redoing the exterior and the front parking places were blocking off because of the scaffolding. I pulled in the first available spot and debated on whether it was worth it to get my umbrella out.

I decided it wasn't worth the hassle and pulled up the hood of my jacket, fastening it tight under my chin, and made a run for it. There was no sidewalk traffic, and I skirted around the edge of the scaffolding managing to get water on the inside of my rain boots, and then I ran up the front steps and opened the door.

The familiar smell of burned coffee and strong disinfectant assaulted my nose, and I wiped my feet on the mat. Sergeant Hill manned the front reception area, and he was the first line of protection between the outside world and the cops that sat in the bullpen behind him.

I was just about to sign in when Jack stuck his head through the employee entrance and said, "Come on back."

Something was up. I waved at Sergeant Hill and then followed Jack through the door, where it locked automatically behind us. He walked back toward his office and I saw Betsy Clement standing by her desk. Betsy wasn't the kind of woman who showed a lot of emotion, but I could've sworn I saw relief on her face.

Betsy hadn't changed in my lifetime, and I had no idea how old she was. Her steel-gray curls were rolled like sausages across the top of her head. She wore a floral-print dress and a soft blue sweater, and her glasses hung from a chain around her neck.

"What's wrong?" I asked, looking back and forth between Jack and Betsy. "You look worried."

"I called the funeral home and Emmy Lu said you were gone," he said. "She said she was busy with a client but she saw when you left on the cameras. Then I tried your cell and it kept going straight to voice mail. That was almost a half hour ago."

I reached in my bag for my cell phone. "Service must be down," I said. "I don't show any missed calls. And it took me a while to get here. I had to go all the way around to the other side of the square to get in. Are you going to tell me what this is about?"

"Betsy got a phone call a while ago from a man who told her to take a message for the sheriff."

"What was the message?" I asked.

Jack handed me a piece of paper, and I saw Betsy's neat handwriting and a word-for-word dictation of the caller.

"The sheriff is messing things up," I read aloud. "Why wouldn't he check his mail? Why would he just leave it on the table? Juliet was the first for you to find. Timing is everything, and now I've had to make adjustments. But it's okay. I can fix it. Just tell him to check his mail."

I trailed off as I finished the last sentence, understanding dawning. "You put the mail on the table when you came home last night. You didn't look at it."

"I know," Jack said.

"Which means someone was watching us," I said, the familiar feeling of panic taking hold. "I felt someone watching. That's why I grabbed the gun. But none of the alarms were triggered."

"You don't have to be on the property to see into the house if you have the right equipment. It would be a long shot, especially with the rain. But not impossible."

"So you're saying some guy was hanging out in a tree looking through binoculars into our house?" I asked.

"More likely from a neighbor's house," Jack

said. "Not everyone has as good of a security system as we do. There's only one spot I can think of that he would've been able to see into our entryway from."

Heresy Road was a secluded street. We didn't have traffic or trick-or-treaters. We didn't do neighborhood barbecues, and there was a good bit of space between each of the houses that had a cliff view. But there was a three-story Victorian across the street from our house—set back from the road—and whoever lived there had let the hedges grow up so it wasn't noticeable unless you were looking for it. I couldn't even say who lived there or that we'd ever met.

"The team is going to meet us at home," Jack said, moving into his office to grab his jacket and keys. "Whatever is in that letter is obviously important to whatever game Juliet's killer is playing. Sheldon was the first one who mentioned he was a Jack the Ripper copycat. I did a little research. The police were sure he committed at least five murders in Whitechapel, but they suspected he was responsible for as many as thirteen. Who knows how many women he has on his agenda. But maybe me not reading the mail kept him from killing another woman last night."

Jack locked his office and then told Betsy, "Let me know if any other calls come through. Someone from IT will be over to set things up so we can record and trace if he calls again. Maybe someone will recognize his voice."

"Don't see how," Betsy said. "It sounded like he'd chewed up and swallowed a bunch of glass."

"I'll be in touch," Jack said. And then he looked at me. "Let's go."

Jack was headed toward the back exit where the gated parking lot was, but I was still standing next to Betsy's desk.

"Jack," I called out, walking fast to catch up with him. I put my hand on his arm so he'd stop and listen.

"We need to hurry," he said. "If he's sending me letters and has a timeline then he's got his next victim picked out. If he hasn't already gotten to her."

"Have you stopped to ask yourself why he'd send the letter to you? To our home?"

"Yeah," he said, moving me toward the back exit. "The original Jack the Ripper sent letters too. He wants to get my attention. And now he's got it."

CHAPTER ELEVEN

JACK DROVE BACK TO THE HOUSE WITH LIGHTS AND sirens. The rain had slowed to a drizzle, but water was still high in places, and we took a roundabout way to get to Anne Boleyn. The water was almost even with the bridge, and Jack drove across it quickly, sending a spray of muddy water up to the windows when we hit a pothole on the other side. We turned right onto Heresy Road, and I noticed police cruisers and Cole's truck pull in behind us and follow all the way to our gate.

Jack hit the remote button and the gate swung open, but I couldn't help but try to get a glimpse at the house across the street as we turned into the driveway.

"Did you call Doug?" I asked.

"Yeah, while I was looking for you," he said.

"I thought we were making things better for him, but now I'm starting to wonder if we've made them worse. This isn't stability. He's lived with us a week and look what's happened. Is this the kind of life we're going to bring our own children into?"

I could feel the tightness in my chest and I pressed a hand there and reminded myself to breathe.

"We're safe here," Jack reminded me. "No one has breached the perimeter and no one has tampered with the alarm or cameras. And Doug knows where the guns are and how to shoot if anyone did pose a threat. This is part of the job. You know that. When I took the oath to lead and protect and serve it automatically painted a target on our back. On yours too."

I let out a slow breath. I knew this already. And it was a decision we'd made together, so I couldn't even blame him for it.

"I know it," I said. "I'm just tired of feeling like it's open season on our home. It doesn't seem to matter what we do to protect it."

"Our home and everything in it are ours to protect. This guy might think he's playing a game, but he doesn't know who his opponents are."

"Carver would normally be right in the middle of this," I said. "Especially knowing that Doug is here."

"Yeah," Jack said, hitting his fist against the wheel. "I've already called him. He's back in DC for a couple of days dealing with some things, but he knows Doug is safe with us. Michelle and the girls also conveniently left to go visit his parents in Florida."

"What's going on?"

"No clue," Jack said. "But I'm afraid to dig too deep without stirring up problems for Carver. I've known him a long time and I trust him. He'll talk to us when he can."

We used the side entrance into the mudroom, and Cole, Martinez, Plank, and Chen followed us inside.

"I'm not going to lie, boss," Martinez said. "Your house got bad juju."

Martinez was a seasoned cop, and had earned the nickname of Mr. GQ because he was always polished up and slick with his clothes and looks. King George had a lot of rural areas and farmland, and there was also a lot of wealth. But you'd never know it by looking at the people. There were no pretenses in King George. We were a hardy bunch who worked hard and tried to make good lives for our families.

So to say Martinez stuck out was an understatement. He wore black slacks and expensive-looking loafers, and he wore a black leather jacket and a gray scarf tied fashionably around his neck. His black hair was well cut and his face was smooth. The ladies loved Martinez and he loved them.

I was starting to think Martinez might not be half wrong about the house having bad juju. Martinez's partner, Lewis, had been killed in our living room by my father. Come to think of it, this was the first time Martinez had been back to our house since that day.

"Maybe we can give your address to the next serial killer," Cole said. "I'm sure Doc would be happy for you to deflect some bad juju your way."

"I don't believe in bad juju," I said, even though I wasn't entirely convinced. "I'm not even sure what juju is."

"I read about this cult the other day that specialized in bad juju," Doug said, bounding down the stairs to meet us. "They ate animal livers and put curses on people. If something has bad juju, believe me, you don't want it."

"Good to know," I said. "Where'd you come from?"

"Biologically or locationally?" Doug asked, making everyone snicker. "I heard you guys come in and thought you might be bringing food."

"Not this time," Jack said, slapping Doug on the shoulder in greeting and then moving to the entryway table where he'd dropped the mail.

Cole moved to stand in front of the windows that flanked each side of the door. The house had been designed to bring the beauty of the outside to the inside as much as possible. There were windows everywhere, and the only ones that had shades were the ones in Jack's office because the sun hit directly and the nature of our work called for privacy, whether we were at home or not.

"You can't see anything from here," Cole said, looking out. "Not without some specialized equipment."

"You have gloves?" Jack asked.

My bag was hanging in the mudroom and I was about to go get it when Chen said, "I've got some," and pulled a pair out of her back pocket.

"Thanks," Jack said, and slipped them on. Then he picked up the mail from the table and rifled through it, tossing down flyers and bills. Until he got to a small envelope. He pulled a knife from his boot and slipped the tip under the flap of the envelope, slicing it open.

"It's got a stamp and it's been postmarked," Jack said. "We can pull saliva from the stamp for DNA. And he handwrote the name and address."

Jack pulled what looked like a postcard from inside the envelope and he held it carefully by the edges.

"It looks old," I said, my brow furrowed in thought. "Like, really old."

It was a plain postcard, maybe four or five inches wide, with a dark red border. The card was yellowed with age and the corners rounded and bent as if someone had held on to it for a long time. There was a red seal of a lion at the top.

"The postcard looks old, but the handwriting is fresh," Jack said. "The ink isn't faded. And the handwriting appears to match what's on the envelope. We can send it to the lab for testing though to make sure."

"What does it say?" Martinez asked, looking over Jack's shoulder. "He's got terrible handwriting."

Jack held it up and said, "It says, *Beware, for I*

found the woman I want. She was unclean. My knife found its mark. I left it for you to find. I need it no more. Until next time, Jack the Ripper."

"I feel like this is one of those times it might be helpful to have Sheldon around," I said.

"That doesn't make sense," Cole said. "Why would he say he doesn't need the knife anymore, and then say until next time?"

"Jack the Ripper left letters to the police," Plank said, drawing everyone's attention.

"I love this kid," Martinez said, squeezing Plank's shoulder. "Just when you think he can't surprise you anymore he comes up with this stuff."

"Or maybe he knows so much because Wachowski loves serial killer documentaries," Chen said, waggling her eyebrows and making Cole and Martinez hoot with laughter.

"He's right," Jack said. "I was doing research this morning."

"I can look them up and we can do an analysis," Doug said. "It shouldn't be too hard to see if there's any similarities."

"Good idea," Jack said.

We moved into the office and Jack scanned the postcard into the computer so it showed up on the whiteboard.

"Work your magic," Jack said to Doug, and Doug sat behind the computer and started typing.

It didn't take long for accompanying images to appear next to the scanned postcard.

"Here you go," Doug said. "He made a point of

getting it as close to the original postcard as he could. Red border and an emblem at the top. Not exactly the same, but pretty close."

"Yeah, pretty close," Jack agreed.

"The original was sent in 1888," Doug said. "I can increase the text so it's easier to read, but this wasn't OG Jack's first contact with the police. But it is the only postcard he sent. The rest are actual letters on stationery. He sent some to the press, and others addressed to a specific policeman."

"He uses the same language," I said. "*Beware.* Then he goes on to say he found the woman he wants, which is almost identical to OG Jack." I decided Doug's moniker was the easiest way to keep all the Jacks straight. "He mentions the knife, but that's where it starts to differ."

"He left us the knife to find," Jack said, studying both of the postcards. "Because he no longer needs it."

"Maybe she was his only victim," Martinez said.

"No," Jack said, shaking his head. "When he called and talked to Betsy he was adamant that I hurry and read his letter because he had an order for things. He said timing was everything."

"Just not with the knife," I said. "It's not like there's a clue in this. It's just a *look what I did* kind of thing. You think he'll send another letter?"

"I'd almost bet on it," Jack said. "Doug, do a reverse address lookup for 1227 Heresy Road. I think we need to pay our neighbors a visit. Maybe they'll cooperate and let us take a look around without getting a warrant."

Doug's fingers flew across the keyboard. "Done. Richard and Jody Burkett. Looks like they've lived there over twenty years. Want me to do a deeper search?"

"Not for now," Jack said. "We won't be long. Lock up after us."

After a short debate, we decided to leave Chen and Plank with Doug, and the rest of us would head across the street to the neighbors' house.

"Speaking of warrants," I said. "You never told me about the ones you put in for this morning."

"I was able to get a warrant for Brian Dunnegan's finances and his home and office. We'll be able to see exactly what he benefits now that Juliet is dead. Peter Trest is another matter."

"What do you mean?" I asked.

"I mean he's delayed the warrant," Jack said. "At least for now. He's friends with the judge. They won't be able to hold it off much longer. He's got no alibi, and the witness saw the killer walking toward the street Trest's studio is on. We'll find something there. And then I'm going to tie his life up in warrants just because I'm annoyed."

My lips twitched in a half smile as we drove past the overgrown shrubs, across a grate and down the gravel driveway to the Burkett's home.

"It's nice," I said. "I guess I've never really taken a good look before." Someone obviously took very good care of the lawn.

It reminded me of an English garden. There was a fountain in the center of a round driveway, and gravel paths lined by different sizes and shapes of shrubbery. There was something purple that looked like spiny troll hair that still managed to look beautiful in the wet and cold.

The house was a three-story Victorian painted olive green with a dark burgundy trim. There were turrets and a widow's walk with a black iron fence. I eyed the windows on the top floor and then looked back across the street toward our house. I couldn't see the house from ground level, but it was possible there was an open view from that high up.

"If it makes you feel better, I have actually met the woman who lives here," Jack said. "She was getting her mail and I stopped to say hello. That was eight years ago."

"You must have made an impression," I said.

"Some people just like their privacy. Would you ever leave the house if you didn't have to go to work?"

"Good point," I said. "I like her already."

We parked behind Cole's truck, and followed him and Martinez up the stairs to the big front porch. There were two rocking chairs and a wreath on the front door, and there was a ceramic cat curled in sleep next to the rocking chair.

Jack pushed the doorbell, and we could hear

the major third echoing through the house, but there was no sound of footsteps coming toward us. Jack rang it one more time, and Cole went back down the stairs and looked to the side of the house.

"There's a black SUV parked in front of the garage," Cole said.

"Maybe the police make them skittish," I said. My phone buzzed and I looked down to see a text from Doug, and my lips twitched. "Doug did a deeper background check on the Burketts. He said he couldn't help himself. Richard Burkett passed away about three years ago, so it's just the wife living here now."

There was something in my gut that screamed not everything was as perfect as it appeared on the outside. Jack rang the bell again and then followed it up with a knock, and I walked over to one of the windows and looked inside.

It was a jolt to the senses, and I couldn't help but gasp at the wide and bulging eyes that stared at me through a clear plastic bag. I could only assume the woman displayed before me was Jody Burkett.

"Jack," I said. "She's dead."

Whatever he heard in my voice had him pulling his weapon, and Cole and Martinez peeled off to move around the side of the house toward the back.

Jack turned the doorknob and found it locked, and then he looked at me and motioned for me to get behind him. His boot made contact with the door and wood splintered as it fell open.

The smell of death and decay greeted us.

CHAPTER TWELVE

"Stay here," Jack said, and started making his way toward the back of the house, clearing the rooms as he went.

I heard the back door open and Jack's voice as he spoke to Cole and Martinez, but I was already moving into the formal living room. The house was immaculate—well taken care of—just like the outside. The room was feminine with dark hardwood floors and the rug and furniture a mix of cream, rose, and moss green. There was a wood-burning fireplace and it was built high with ash and the remainder of a burned log.

The placement of the furniture in the room was off somehow, as if everything had been pushed back just a little bit to make room for what sat at the center.

The killer had staged her so she'd be seen from the windows on the front porch. He'd opened the blinds and placed a hard wooden dining chair with arms in the center of the rug, and he'd faced it toward the windows. The woman's clothes had been removed and her wrists and ankles had been zip-tied to the chair.

There were contusions and abrasions around the neck, and not from the plastic bag that had been zip-tied around her throat. It looked like rope burn or something similar, but I wouldn't know for sure until I got her into the lab.

I looked around on the ground and found no signs of debris or rope he might have used to torture her—the only thing on the rug was what the body had released in death.

I didn't want to touch her yet—not until crime scene could come in and document—but I moved around her cataloging what I could see with the naked eye.

"You okay?" Jack asked, coming back into the room.

"Yeah, I'm fine," I said, not taking my eyes off the victim. "Any sign of him?"

"No, he's long gone," Jack said. "We found his hole up in the third-floor tower. There's a telescope up there, and it's pointed straight at our windows. Fortunately, it's only the front entryway you can see from that angle."

"She's been dead for a while," I said. "Look at the lividity in her feet and along the bottom of her thighs and buttocks." I pointed to the purplish bruising where the blood had pooled. "That puts time of death at minimum around ten to twelve hours, but I'm guessing more. I'll be able to tell you more once I can get a temperature read."

"I called Chen and she's on her way over with your bag," Jack said.

"Thanks," I said. "Look at the strangulation marks around the neck."

"What about them?" Jack said.

"There's different striations. Different angles. He strangled her several times."

"What?" Jack asked. "And then brought her back and did it again?"

"That's what it looks like," I said. "Torture."

"Sexual assault?" he asked.

"It's definitely sexual in nature," I said. "He took the time and trouble to undress her." I took a UV light from my bag and turned it on, pointing first at the victim and then on the floor surrounding her. There were three different areas that lit up. "Seminal fluid. Does this crime scene look familiar to you?"

"As callous as it sounds, the killer didn't use an original idea," Jack said.

"That's what I'm talking about."

"What do you mean?" he asked.

"I don't know," I said, my brow furrowed. "I need to think on it. But there's something."

"Come upstairs with me while you're waiting on CSI to finish up," Jack said.

I wanted to tell Jack there wasn't a snowball's chance in hell I would go upstairs with him. I didn't want to put myself in the killer's shoes. Look through the same telescope he'd had his eye pressed against while he looked in our windows.

I must have hesitated too long because Jack said, "You don't have to."

"No, I'm fine," I said.

I took off my leather gloves and shoved them in my pocket because my hands were hot and sweaty, and I took out a pair of latex gloves from my bag, donning them instead.

The carpet runner was worn and the wooden stairs creaked beneath our feet as we climbed higher to the third floor. I didn't realize until we got there that the tower was actually a fourth, more narrow flight of stairs.

"Yikes," I said, as the walls seemed to close in. "Hello, claustrophobia."

"It doesn't last long," Jack said, and pushed open a wooden door at the top of the stairs. He went in first, because there was no room for me to go in before him. "Brace yourself."

I didn't know what he meant until I walked inside and got a good look of the room. "There's not a lot of things in this world that give me night-mares," I said.

"I know," Jack agreed.

Masks lined the walls—clown, phantom, jester —all shapes and colors and sizes. There were framed posters of plays and a collection of *Playbills*.

And there were a dozen or more Styrofoam heads with wigs on them.

"If there are creepy dolls I'm out of here," I said. "You can just ship all my clothes to Aruba."

"I haven't seen any dolls yet," he said, smiling. "But if I find any we'll go to Aruba together. We don't even need clothes."

There was a single window in the room and there was a padded bench seat beneath it. But the window was open, and the cushion had been soaked through. I looked down at the floor and saw the wood and rug were wet.

"It's been open for a while," I said. "Lot of water collected in here."

I took note of the rocking chair pulled close to the telescope. "Wanted to be comfortable."

I stopped just short of the telescope and held my breath, feeling the pulse throbbing in my neck. I could see the structure of our house lit up by the lights around the perimeter and on the inside. I put my eye up close to the telescope, careful not to touch it, knowing exactly what I'd see.

The familiar entry table and scraped hardwood floors came into view. I could see all the way through to the living area and the floor-to-ceiling windows that looked out over the trees and the Potomac.

"Well," I said, taking a step back, my boots sloshing on the carpet. "I think that settles it. Bad juju. Maybe we should just burn it down and start over."

"I'm thinking the insurance adjusters might have something to say about that," Jack said. "Look, there's the crime scene techs."

I watched the van pull into the drive with all the other myriad of cop cars. We went back downstairs and let them in and then waited while they put down numbered markers and took photographs of anything relevant. And then they dusted for prints, hoping to find anything that didn't belong to the victim.

"I called Lily and Sheldon in," I said. "They can get her transported and set up for the autopsy. I should be able to finish it by tonight. Everything is jumbled in my mind. How is this case like our Jack the Ripper murder? Obviously, the guy who killed Juliet wrote the copycat letter and wanted us to find the victim here. But this murder is nothing like the Jack the Ripper murder."

"No," Jack said. "We've got two female victims. Both Caucasian. Juliet was in her late thirties. This woman seems to be quite a bit older. Juliet lived in Newcastle and this victim in Bloody Mary. But they have a killer in common. Why?"

I didn't have an answer.

"You're up, Doc," the lead crime scene tech said, nodding as he passed by.

I looked at her hands first. Feeling the loosened joints and skin and looking at her fingernails. And then I pressed along her ribs and the thickest part of her waist.

"She's completely out of rigor," I said. "And you

can see the cuticles have started pulling back from the nails. The skin is shrinking." I dug in my bag for the digital thermometer. "She's room temperature. What's the thermostat set on?"

Jack walked into the hallway to check and said, "Seventy degrees."

I did the math in my head and then calculated the completed stages of rigor. "At least twenty-four hours. Could be as much as forty-eight, but I don't think so. We don't have any insect activity yet. Twenty-four to thirty-six is the best guestimate. What were we doing twenty-four to thirty-six hours ago?"

Jack looked at his watch. "It's just after two o'clock. We were leaving Taco Joe's," he said. "You'd already finished Juliet's autopsy."

"So thirty-six hours ago it was two in the morning," I said. "Juliet was freshly dead."

"He killed Juliet and then came here sometime in the next few hours and killed Jody Burkett," Jack said, nodding.

"Which means he probably already had Jody held captive."

"Timeline," Jack said. "He was insistent about the timeline when he talked to Betsy. He's moving fast and he needed me to catch up."

That gave me an uneasy feeling in the pit of my stomach. I didn't like it when murderers decided to include us in on their game.

"Did you find an ID for her?" I asked. "Let's make sure this is Jody Burkett."

"I can identify her," Jack said. "This is the woman I talked to."

"Okay," I said. "I'm not seeing any other marks or wounds on her. I'll test for sexual assault once I get back to the lab. The probability is high. Maybe we can get some DNA."

I took a sharp pair of shears from my bag and carefully cut the zip tie around her throat and removed the plastic bag. Jack had an evidence bag already open and waiting for me, and I dropped it inside.

The front door opened again and Sheldon and Lily came inside with a gurney.

"I'm telling you she liked you," Lily said. "That's why she gave you her phone number."

"I don't know," Sheldon said. "She told me she had questions about my *Lord of the Rings* memorabilia. It's an extensive collection. I've had lots of people interested in seeing it. I've got to be careful though because one time a guy tried to steal my mithril shirt replica."

"Believe me," Lily said. "She doesn't want to see your collection. She's interested in you. Call her and ask her out."

"Maybe I could text," he said. "Where would we go?"

"I'm glad you found a date, Sheldon," I said. "But I'd like to wrap this up. This is our fourth body in less than forty-eight hours."

"Five if you count Louise Chalmers," Sheldon

said. "The hospital finally got her delivered. Only one spot left in the cooler."

"Right," I said. "I'm just finishing up here."

I ran a finger over each of the strangulation marks. "I'm counting at least three different ligature marks," I said. "That kind of torture takes time. He strangles her to the point of passing out and then waits for her to revive so he can do it again. She'd be wishing for death."

"No one knows she's here," Jack said. "Lives alone. Keeps to herself. He comes and goes as he pleases. Tortures her for a bit and then goes and kills Juliet. Comes back and tortures her some more."

"You think there's a possibility one of our cameras might have picked him up coming or going?"

"Worth a shot," he said. "I can have Doug start looking through the camera feed."

"Like you said, he's on a timeline," I said. "It's time to move on to his next victim, so he puts the plastic bag over her head and finishes her off."

I cut the zip ties at her wrists and bagged both of her hands, just in case she happened to get a swipe in before he incapacitated her. I called Lily and Sheldon over with the gurney and then cut the straps around her ankles.

"This is weird," Sheldon said. "What are the odds there'd be so many copycat murders?"

Jack put a restraining hand on Sheldon's shoulder and asked, "What do you mean?"

"Oh," he said, blinking owlishly. "I'm kind of a serial killer aficionado. I know all kinds of things about them. We should watch a marathon sometime. They've always got these great documentaries. I thought you would know all about them."

"I live this life on a daily basis," Jack said. "The last thing I want to do is go home and watch serial killer documentaries."

"Oh," Sheldon said. "I guess that makes sense."

"Focus, Sheldon," I said. "Tell us about the copycat murders."

"Well, first you've got Jack the Ripper. That one's pretty obvious. And then you've got the random shooting at the theater. The guy was even driving a yellow car." Sheldon looked at us expectantly.

"Spell it out for us, Sheldon," I said.

"Son of Sam," he said. "No rhyme or reason to his kills. Just picked them out and opened fire. He drove a yellow car."

Jack met my gaze and I knew what he was thinking. We'd not even considered the shooting to be related. Why would we have? But had we missed something important because we hadn't seen the connection?

"What about this one?" Jack asked.

Sheldon looked down at the woman, pity in his eyes. "BTK," he said. "Bind, torture, kill."

"God Almighty," Cole said from the doorway. He must have come in while Sheldon had been explaining. "He's moving fast."

"He's got a timeline," Jack said.

"Let's get her bagged and loaded and back to the funeral home," I said. "We need to run this guy to ground before he strikes again. He killed four people yesterday. And today is already halfway over."

CHAPTER THIRTEEN

"WE COULD REALLY USE CARVER ON THIS," I TOLD Jack as we watched Lily and Sheldon drive away with Jody Burkett.

"Yeah, well, we've got the younger version," Jack said. "He's running deep backgrounds on all the victims to see if there's a connection between any of them. Let's go talk to Bruno Corelli and let Doug see what he can dig up. All I can think is that every hour that passes makes it more likely he's killed again."

I'd been having those thoughts too, and it was those thoughts that got in the way of logical thinking.

"Betsy said Bruno Corelli works as a supervisor at the waste management company in King George," Jack said. "He should be there now."

"I guess acting didn't pay off like he thought it would," I said.

Jack grunted and turned onto Highway 3—also

known as Kings Highway—and I pulled out my phone to read more about the copycat murders, and why our killer would have picked these specific serial killers to emulate.

A beam of sunlight glared off my screen and it took me a second to realize what it was. I looked up and saw the rain had stopped, and the sun was attempting to make an appearance.

"Oh, thank you, Jesus," I said. "I was starting to worry we should've been looking for an ark to jump on."

"Forecast says the rain is supposed to clear up," Jack said. "No telling what the mess is going to look like once the water recedes a little. Reports coming in from the guys are that there's been quite a bit of vehicle damage, and several homes along the shallow banks that took on water."

"What about your parents?" I asked.

"They're good. They've been busy in the green-houses getting seeds germinated so they're ready to plant in the spring. Mom says we should come to dinner next Sunday."

I loved Jack's mom. She'd been more like a mother to me growing up than my own had. Jack's parents owned one of the remaining three hundred tobacco farms in the state of Virginia. The Lawson farm had been in his family for generations, and they'd held on to it with everything they had once regulations and taxes and federal restrictions had started making things more difficult to survive.

"Why would he copycat?" I asked, my thoughts

going back to the killer. "This is not a short notice operation. Victorian week obviously played a part. He waited for the right time so it would fit the scenario he wanted to imitate. And that was the starting pistol. You know he's got a playbook. The crimes he wants to commit and how he wants to do it."

"He copycats because he doesn't see himself as having the capability of being an original," Jack said. "He wants to show us what he can do—perform for us in a way—but he's got low self-esteem. He wants recognition and affirmation. Someone like that screams mommy or daddy wounds."

"Perform," I said softly.

I called Doug and put him on speaker so Jack could hear too.

"I just got started," Doug said by way of greeting. "Give a guy a break. Pizza delivery is back up and running by the way. I needed some fuel."

"Tell me about Jody Burkett," I said.

"Already have her pulled up," he said around a mouth full of pizza. "Jody Pickering Burkett. She's a Newcastle native. Sixty-four years old. Married to Richard Burkett for forty years before he passed away from cancer a few years back. She's a retired teacher. Looks like the husband was a financial adviser."

"What did she teach and where?" I asked, looking at Jack. I could tell he was already a step ahead of me.

"Let's see," Doug said. "Newcastle high school. She taught theater."

"Thanks, Doug," Jack said. "See if any of our other victims had a connection to Jody Burkett."

"Will do," Doug said. "How long are Plank and Chen going to babysit me?"

"Until we can make sure the serial killer on the loose is tired of looking in our windows," Jack said. "We're making a stop and then we'll be back home tonight. Be good for the babysitters."

Doug snickered before he hung up.

"So the common thread is theater," I said. "Juliet is an actress. A frequent face at the Curtain Call. She's chosen by the killer because she fits the Jack the Ripper narrative. A woman of ill repute. And the killer dresses like the master. He leaves the murder weapon because he doesn't need it again. Just like he told you in the letter. He won't kill like that again."

Jack nodded in agreement and said, "Then we've got the Son of Sam at the movie theater. He's comfortable at the theater. Those are his people. That's his home and he keeps going back to it. I believe the victims were completely random, and he was just fulfilling his part in the play. He became David Berkowitz, just like he'd become Jack the Ripper. Doug told us the shooter had curly hair and weird sideburns. No facial hair like the witness saw for Jack the Ripper."

"And then he left the gun in the glove box because he doesn't need it anymore," I said. "And then somewhere in between Jack the Ripper and Son of Sam, he becomes the BTK Killer." I was scrolling through my phone, digging for information, and there was one thing that stuck out.

"Have you checked the mail today?" I asked.

"It still hadn't come by the time we left," Jack said. "I've got Plank and Chen looking out for it."

"All three of the original killers sent letters to the police," I said. "He's got a whole cast of characters in whatever warped play he's created in his mind. And it looks like we're on the playbill."

Jack's lips pressed together in a tight line and he pressed a button on the steering wheel. "Call Plank," he commanded, and the phone started to ring.

"Sheriff," Plank said.

"Has the mail come yet?" Jack asked.

"Yes, sir," Plank said. "It just arrived. Chen and I both looked through, but there was nothing but ads and flyers. Nothing handwritten or addressed specifically to you."

"Okay, thanks," Jack said and disconnected. And then he immediately dialed the next number and Betsy Clement came on the line.

"Sheriff's office," she said. "Betsy Clement speaking. How can I help you?"

"Betsy, it's Jack. Has the mail come today?"

"Not yet. Is there anything I should be looking for?"

"Look for any letters addressed to me," he said. "It'll be handwritten. Tell whoever is going through the mail to put on gloves first. We're just pulling up to the waste plant in King George to talk with a person of interest. I'll touch base once we're done here."

"10-4," she said and hung up.

The waste management plant was over by the railroad tracks, and it was several large industrial buildings surrounded by a tall chain-link fence. There was a gated entrance and a guard stepped out as we approached.

"Can I help you?" the guard asked. He was an older man, probably in his sixties, with a shock of silver hair and a pleasant, round face and twinkling blue eyes.

"Bruno Corelli?" Jack asked.

The guard nodded and reached for his clipboard, running his finger down the page until he found the name. "He's in building two." He pointed us to a building on the left. "Should be able to find him there. He's still clocked in."

"Appreciate it," Jack said, and waved as the gate opened for us.

"I've never been to the waste plant before," I said. "I thought it would smell worse."

"There's so many chemicals here you'll be lucky if you can smell at all by the time we leave," Jack said, pulling into a parking spot outside of building two.

"Look at the way the sun is shining off the metal roof," I said. "Isn't it glorious."

"I think you're waterlogged," Jack said. "Sounds like it's time for a beach trip."

"Stop talking sexy like that to me," I said. "I can't be held responsible for what I'll do."

"You're so easy," he said, squeezing my shoulder.

"When it comes to you, I'm always easy," I said. "Now put on your mean face so Bruno takes us seriously."

"I don't have a mean face," Jack said.

I laughed. "You don't really think that, do you? You can be a scary guy. And you have cop face."

"Cop face?" he asked, arching a brow.

"You know how you can always tell who's a cop in the room. It's the eyes. You've got good eyes. But you can be intimidating when you want to be."

"Do I intimidate you?" he asked.

"No," I said, grinning at him. "But I'll let you practice on me later."

Even if I hadn't already seen Bruno Corelli's driver's license picture, I would've been able to pick him out of a lineup. If anyone looked like a Bruno, it was him.

He was several inches over six feet and built like a bear. His shoulders were broad and his biceps well defined, but he'd gone a little soft in the middle. He looked like a man who enjoyed a beer or five. His hair was dark and his beard was close cropped, and he looked comfortable in a red flannel shirt and jeans.

"Mr. Corelli?" Jack asked, moving his jacket aside so his badge was visible.

"Yeah?" Bruno asked.

"Can we talk to you a few minutes? It's about Juliet Dunnegan."

He looked at us nervously and then swallowed. "Sure. Come on back to my office. I can take a few minutes."

The office was made of tin siding with a white door that looked like it had been kicked a few times and a window with cheap blinds hanging haphazardly. On the door was a placard that said *Waste Supervisor—Antonio Corelli*.

He cleared his throat and said, "I heard what happened to Juliet. Everyone in the company was talking about it. We were all there. I just don't see how it could have happened. There were people everywhere."

"The company?" I asked.

"The regular cast at the Curtain Call," he said. "We do five new plays every year and *A Christmas Carol* every December. We audition for the parts, so we're never in the same roles. I was working sets for this last one." He kind of laughed and then pointed to his body. "I'm not exactly built like an English lord. Sorry about the mess."

He moved stacks of papers and files off two metal chairs and then he rolled his desk chair to the side so we could see each other face-to-face.

"You said you were working sets?" Jack asked. "What does that mean?"

"I'm the heavy lifter behind the scenes, rolling sets into place and making sure everything is ready for the next scene. It's an important job. Stressful."

"Did you see Juliet after the play was over?" Jack asked.

"Not really," he said. "Things are kind of crazy then. People are moving and family members are coming backstage. Especially on closing night. The last time I saw her was after the last curtain call. She was heading to her dressing room, and she gave me a quick wave. It was real quick. We didn't even speak." He swallowed again and clasped his hands together. "It's hard to think that was the last time. She was so alive. Smiling and excited. Everyone has that glow after a final performance. It's a lot of work."

"What did you do after the play was over?" Jack asked.

"On the last night everyone leaves the mess for the next day cleanup and we all go out and get drunk," he said, shrugging. "It's tradition. But I had to be here at work at eight in the morning, so I took a raincheck. I went home instead."

"Can anyone verify that?" Jack asked.

"I don't know," he said, shrugging. "Maybe some of the guys saw me leave. I told them I couldn't go with them. I've made that mistake before and I learned my lesson. Got fired from a job once for partying all night before I came into work."

"What was your relationship like with Juliet?" Jack asked.

Bruno blew out a breath and crossed his arms over his chest, leaning back in his chair. "How much time do you have?" he asked, trying to smile. "It was complicated."

"Because of all the other men in her life?" I asked.

"No, nothing like that," he said. "We dated in high school some, so we had a history. And sometimes people you have a history with are just comfortable. Juliet had a rough upbringing. Dad was an alcoholic and her mom walked out on them Juliet's freshman year of high school. I think she was always searching for a knight in shining armor to kind of carry her away. You know what I mean?"

"Yeah," Jack said softly. "I know what you mean."

"She would have married me right out of high school if I'd asked her," he said. "She'd hinted at it a time or two, but I wasn't ready for marriage. Things kind of cooled off between us after that and she said she was going to LA to be an actress. She always loved performing. And she was good at it. Better than me. I only ever joined theater because the girls were pretty. And then I found I liked it too. Weird how that works, huh?"

"She left town?" I asked, keeping him on track.

"Sure did," he said. "Packed her bags and snuck in my window the night she left. She didn't tell me she was leaving. I just thought she was over her pout and wanted to pick up where we'd left off. The next morning there was a goodbye note on my dresser. I probably kept that thing ten years before I threw it away. I always expected to see her in some commercial or movie someday, but I never did."

"She obviously came back home," Jack said.

"Yeah, she spent about ten years in Hollywood before she came back," he said. "It looked like it had been a hard ten years. I was already involved with the Curtain Call. That was before Trest bought it and renovated the place. So she kind of fit right back into the fold when she moved back. She waited tables and did her thing. But boy, she could con a conman. Always looked like she had money even though she didn't have two nickels to rub together. Was good with makeup and hairstyles. She met that jerk she's married to pretty quick after moving back and she didn't waste any time getting a proposal from him."

"What about the two of you?" Jack asked. "Did you take up where you left off?"

"A time or two," he said. "But ten years is a long time and things had changed. We both knew it. But like I said, we had a history, and sometimes that's nice."

"A source told us you two were hooked up right before she started dating Peter Trest," Jack said. "The source told us you were jealous and overbearing. That you fought."

He laughed, but there was no humor in it. "You're kidding, right?"

"You tell us," Jack said.

"The theater world is kind of incestuous, for lack of a better term. Everyone gets passed around. It's just the culture. We're dramatic and like to pretend that we suffer for our art, or that we're never appreciated for our true genius. It's no secret that Juliet and I have taken each other for a spin off and on over the last twenty something years. But I wasn't jealous. What I was was pissed. And yeah, we fought. I was her safety net. Every time she moved on from one man to the next, she'd stop by my place so I could patch up her broken heart and she could move on to the next guy. I was sick of it. She's kept me tied up in knots since I was fifteen years old."

"That must have made you angry," I said sympathetically.

"Oh, yeah," he said. "I'd like to have a life at some point. Maybe settle down and have a kid or two. And I told her that, but she didn't care. She told me she wanted to try again, just the two of us, and see if we could make it work this time. She even popped out a tear or two so it looked like she was sincere."

"She wasn't?"

"Hell no," Bruno said. "There wasn't a sincere bone in her body. I felt sorry for the girl she was, but the woman she became was a narcissistic she-devil. I told her I was done with her and not to show up at my door again because she wasn't satisfied with someone else. I told her to go home to her husband and try to make that work for a change instead of ruining some other guy's life. We got loud, I guess, and she threw a couple of things at me and the neighbor called the cops. By the time they got there she'd already left."

"And then she started dating Peter Trest?" Jack asked.

Bruno had this far-off look in his eyes, and he was staring at the wall to my left. I wasn't sure he was going to answer.

"That's what I heard," he said. "I took a break from the Curtain Call for a month or so, but when I came back she was hooked up with him. We didn't really have reason to talk much over the last couple of months. She seemed happy for the first time since I can remember. She was kind of getting her cake and eating it too between her husband and Trest."

"Can you think of anyone who'd want to hurt Juliet?" Jack asked.

"I don't know," he said. "Not really. For all Juliet's faults, people liked her. She was fun. The life of the party. Even the guys whose hearts she broke a little still liked her. She was never mean when she broke things off with a guy, and they usually stayed friends or at least cordial. She had a couple of angry wives come at her a time or two. A man's marital status never mattered much to her. She always said if they didn't care about their vows then she didn't know why she should."

"Did you know she was pregnant?" Jack asked.

It was the first time I felt like we were getting a real emotion from him and not something rehearsed like a line from a play. His mouth dropped open in surprise and he shook his head slowly.

"No way," he said. "Juliet couldn't have kids. That's impossible."

"It's not," I assured him. "She was about four months along."

His eyes narrowed and there was a flash of rage in them so vivid I could most definitely see him killing Juliet in anger. Someone who had an intimate relationship with her. Someone who'd been used by her over and over again.

"We can do a paternity test and see if the child was yours," I told him.

The anger drained and he just looked sad. "What's the point? She's gone. There's no baby. It is what it is. I loved her a long time ago. I'll remember the girl I knew instead of the woman. It's better that way."

"One more question," Jack said. "Do you know Jody Burkett?"

A look of confusion came across his face, but he nodded. "Of course I do," he said. "Mrs. Burkett was our theater teacher. She retired a few years ago. Why? What's that got to do with anything?"

"She's dead," Jack said. "Murdered in her own home."

"What? What the hell is happening?"

Jack and I got to our feet.

"Am I a suspect?" Bruno asked.

"I wouldn't leave town, Mr. Corelli," Jack said. "We might have more questions for you."

CHAPTER FOURTEEN

"ANY WORD FROM BETSY?" I ASKED AS WE GOT BACK into the Tahoe.

"Not yet," he said. "I'm sure the postal service is running behind with the weather. What do you say we pay a surprise visit to Peter Trest? Our warrant might be delayed, but maybe he'll let us in for cooperation's sake so he doesn't look guilty."

"Guys like that don't care if they look guilty," I said. "I guarantee he's already got expensive lawyers on standby. But we're thinking along the same lines. He's a man intrigued by the theater. He loves it enough to have bought the Curtain Call and then spent millions on renovations. He's an artist. I wonder if he's got experience with makeup."

"He fits the build on the man the witness saw," Jack said. "A whole lot better than Bruno Corelli. But we can't rule Corelli out. The witness said it was dark and the guy was kind of hunched over.

And the description Doug gave was of a bigger guy, fuller in the face."

"That still doesn't explain the beard," I said.

"If makeup artists can glue a beard on Gandalf, I'm sure it can be done to someone like Bruno Corelli."

"Aww, look at you with your nerd reference," I said, batting my eyelashes. "You learned so much during the Campus-Con case."

Jack rolled his eyes. "Everyone knows Gandalf. Knowing the name is like knowing who Santa Claus is. It hardly counts as nerd lore."

My lips twitched with laughter. "Methinks thou dost protest too much."

Cole's call interrupted our discussion. "Thank God," Jack said. "What's up, Cole?"

"We're wrapping things up at the crime scene," he said. "Should be out of here in the next hour and we'll head to your place. You're buying dinner."

Jack smiled. "Don't I always?"

"I can't buy for everyone on my lowly salary," Cole said. "That's why they pay you the big bucks."

"Oh, good," Jack said. "I was wondering where that extra money was supposed to go. I've just been tossing it out the window. You got anything else for me?"

"Yeah, I called to tell you I got the run on the yellow Ford Fusion. Registered to Donald Lightfoot. It's his daughter's car. She's sixteen and left her purse and keys inside. Apparently, she has a bad habit of doing that."

"He would've known her habits," Jack said. "He watched her just like he did his victims because he needed the car. Put a deputy on the girl and her family just in case he has her targeted as a potential victim."

"Already done," Cole said. "I ran the dad as a precaution, but he's clean. He reported his daughter's car stolen on Sunday morning before they left for church, and then they went to Richmond to have dinner at his in-laws' and didn't get back until late."

"We just finished talking to Bruno Corelli," Jack said. "He and Juliet went to high school together. And guess who their theater teacher was?"

"Liza Minnelli," Cole said.

I snickered and glanced at Jack. We'd all been working long hours, and there was always a point where you either got a little delirious or a little annoyed with everyone you worked with. Cole and Jack apparently fit into each of those categories.

Jack pressed his lips together and narrowed his eyes at me. "Jody Burkett."

"Even better," Cole said. "That's an unfortunate coincidence for Mr. Corelli."

"It gets better," Jack said. "There's a possibility Juliet's baby was his."

Cole whistled. "And look who just moved into the prime suspect spot."

"Yeah, except for one problem," I said. "Bruno Corelli doesn't fit the witness description for Jack the Ripper. And he doesn't fit Doug's description of Son of Sam."

"Makeup, wigs, costumes," Cole said.

"He's built like a lumberjack and has a nice beard," I said. "That would be one heck of a transformation."

"Stranger things have happened with makeup and actors. Look at Gandalf. Just pull on the beard next time and see if it comes off."

Jack looked at me and grinned, his point made. "Good idea on the beard pulling," Jack said. "It's been a while since we had a lawsuit."

"The city attorneys don't have anything better to do," Cole said.

"We're headed to go see Peter Trest," Jack said. "We talked to him Monday morning. He had every opportunity to come and go as he pleased while he kept Jody Burkett captive and tortured her. He owns the theater, and he's the right height and build. Facial hair, sideburns, wigs. All easily accessible for a man in his position. And he told his assistant he was holing up in his studio to paint all weekend. Covering all his bases."

"Plus, you just don't like him," I chimed in.

"That too," Jack agreed. "And I get annoyed when judges delay warrants because of who their friends are."

"Ahh," Cole said. "You must have gotten Judge Whittmer."

"Bingo," Jack said. "Let me know if you find anything interesting."

"Will do," Cole said. "We're combing the exterior now while the rain has stopped."

They disconnected and we were driving around the park toward Danbury Street and Trest's gallery when Betsy's name lit up on the dashboard screen.

"Betsy," Jack said.

"Got your letter," she said. "Just like you said. Someone wrote your name on the front in big block letters."

"Put it in an evidence bag and lock it in your drawer unless you see Cole or Martinez," Jack said. "We're in Newcastle and headed back your direction. Stay alert, Betsy."

"I'm a bullfrog," she said and hung up.

I snorted out a laugh and looked at Jack. "She's a bullfrog? What the heck does that mean?"

Jack grinned and pulled into a parking space across the street from the gallery. All the businesses were open as usual and afternoon traffic was back to normal.

"Bullfrogs can go months at a time without sleeping so they can stay alert," he said.

"Betsy the bullfrog," I said. "That's a new one."

"She's outlasted forty years of sheriffs," Jack said. "Must be working for her."

Jack opened the gallery door for me and we went inside to the comfortable warmth. Now that I knew what Trest's beginning of life series was, all I could see were the tiny sperm all over his canvases.

"Disturbing," I said.

Jack countered. "Please don't ever buy that for my office."

We could hear the hushed voices coming from another gallery room, and we wound our way through the room featuring King George woodworkers until we found the source.

Lina stood stiffly with her arms crossed over her chest and her chin defiant. She wore a skintight sleeveless sheath in cherry red and matching heels, and I was envious of the definition in her shoulders and arms. She looked like she could take care of herself.

Rick stood facing her, with his back to us, in a similar outfit he'd worn the day before—pressed khakis and a blue-and-white check button-down, only this time he'd added a navy sweater vest. He held his jacket over his arm.

"I'm sorry, Rick," Lina said. "I don't know what else to tell you."

Rick made a sound of frustration and paced back and forth like a caged lion. "He can't do this to people."

"Oh, Sheriff Lawson," Lina said, once she noticed us. Her brow furrowed in brief irritation, but the lines smoothed out and she gave us a polite smile. "I'm sorry if you've come by to see Mr. Trest, but he's not in today."

Rick rolled his eyes at that and kept up his pacing.

"That's okay," Jack said cordially. "We'll just catch him at home."

"Yeah, good luck with that," Rick said. "The almighty Trest has spoken and he's decided to take off for an unspecified mourning period. That's what you get when the owner has a god complex and likes to pretend everyone else on earth is just a puppet on a string. It's not like he loved Juliet. He could barely remember her name half the time. But women don't seem to care. They just throw themselves at him anyway."

"Is Mr. Trest planning to leave town?" Jack asked, directing the question at Lina.

Her mouth dropped open in surprise at the question. "I...I couldn't say," she said. "Mr. Trest moves to his own whims. He messaged me late last night and told me he needed to take some time to mourn the loss of Juliet." Then she gave an arch look at Rick. "They were very close."

Rick finally stopped his pacing and faced us. "And he called *me* last night to say that the theater should remain closed indefinitely. This is just typical. We've got cast and staff and plays already lined up, tickets presold. But he doesn't care about anyone but himself. He's just going to hole up somewhere for God knows how long, and then when he decides to grace us with his presence again he'll wonder why things aren't running as smoothly as he left them."

"Rick," Lina said warningly.

Rick turned on Lina. "No, I'm not doing it. I'm not putting all those people out of work. Get on the phone and talk to him. I know you have his direct contact."

"Mr. Trest is entitled to his privacy, and these are his businesses to run how he sees fit," Lina said. "If you're not satisfied you can find employment elsewhere."

"I've been at the Curtain Call long before Trest came along," Rick said. "There are people involved besides that self-centered jerk. Next time you talk to him tell him I'm running things as usual. He made me the manager and that's what I plan on doing."

Rick nodded at us and then walked out swiftly.

"Is there anything else I can do for you?" Lina asked, obviously wanting us to follow Rick out the door.

"Yes," Jack said. "Let Mr. Trest know that this is an ongoing murder investigation and he's not to leave town. We still have questions."

Lina nodded stiffly, and Jack and I turned around and headed back toward the front. Rick was waiting for us there.

"He's really not a great artist," Rick said, pointing to the beginning of life paintings hung on the wall. "Who would want that in their living room? It's creepy. I think he's got issues with his birth mom. I read somewhere she abandoned him and his grandmother raised him. I'm sorry I lost my temper back there."

"It sounds like you're just looking out for your people," Jack said. "It's understandable."

"We're a family," Rick said. "I know some people don't understand, but we really are. At first, we all just did it because we love the theater. We'd put on these plays in the park. Someone would write the script, and everyone would pitch in sewing costumes and helping with sets. But over the last several years the theater has been turning a profit, so we've been able to have full-time staff, and the cast gets a stipend. It only works if everyone is working together. Do you know how hard my job is? I'm dealing with actors and theater people on a daily basis. It's constant drama and feelings and tantrums and lovers' quarrels. It's exhausting."

"Why do you do it?" I asked.

"Because I love it," he said, blowing out a breath. "Ever since I was a kid and saw *Bye Bye Birdie* onstage. I was hooked. But I found out early on that my talents are best used off

stage. I'm good at what I do. It's not a big important job, and I don't make a lot of money. But it was never about that. It's about making the stars shine as bright as they can, and entertaining the people at the same time."

Rick moved to open the front door and held it for us so we could pass through. I turned my face up to the sunlight, appreciating the change, even though the cold was still bitter.

"So what are you going to do?" I asked.

"I'm going to call a staff meeting and get things ready for rehearsal tomorrow," he said. "He made me manager, so I'm going to manage until he fires me or we run out of money to pay the staff."

"We talked to Bruno Corelli," Jack said. "He couldn't think of anyone who might want to harm Juliet. What about you? Can you think of anyone?"

"Not really," Rick said. "There was a lady that interrupted rehearsal once. I think her name was Brenda. Maybe Brynlee. I don't remember. It was three or four years ago. But she'd found out Juliet and her husband were having an affair and kind of went off her rocker. Came into the theater during practice with a baseball bat. A couple of the guys tackled her to the ground, and then she screamed at Juliet for a bit and ran off."

"Nothing ever came of it?" Jack asked. "No police report filed?"

"Nah, Juliet didn't want to mess with it. She didn't want it to look bad for her husband. She always knew where her bread was buttered. She just shook it off and went about rehearsal like nothing had happened. That was one of her best performances that night. Really revved her up."

"Can you think of any cast or staff members who were close with Jody Burkett?" Jack asked.

Rick laughed and looked at us like we we'd just fallen off the turnip truck. "Are you kidding? Jody Burkett is an acting legend. Everyone knows her around here. She does master classes all the time for the cast. She spent some time working in New York off-Broadway, so she's really taken our performances up a notch. Why? You don't suspect Jody could have anything to do with Juliet's murder, do you? She's a tough old bat, but she could never hurt a fly."

"We found Jody Burkett's body earlier today," Jack said. "We believe she was murdered by the same man who killed Juliet."

Rick paled and took a step back. "Oh my God," he said. "I can't believe it. Everyone is going to be devastated when they find out." Then he looked at us in a panic. "Are we all in danger? Do you think we're being targeted?"

"It's a possibility," Jack said.

"I need to call everyone together," he said. "If we're in danger we need to stick close to each other. Watch each other's backs. That's what we do best. And leave it to Mr. Trest to hide himself away while all hell breaks loose. Selfish bastard." He put on his jacket, realizing he was still holding it. "I'm sorry. I've got to go."

We watched him walk across the street and back toward the theater.

"Let's get back to the sheriff's office," Jack said. "I want to take a look at that letter. This guy has us running in circles, and it's really starting to piss me off."

"It's because he's moving so fast," I said. "It's hard to get ahold of something and run it to ground when you keep having to go to crime scenes and process another dead body. We just need to go home and spend some time in front of the murder board. Something will click into place."

"I hope you're right," Jack said.

"And just so we're clear," I said. "I'm on Brenda/Brynlee's side. Only I'd be coming after you with the bat instead of the other woman."

Jack grinned. "So noted." He turned on his lights and sped back to the sheriff's office.

The sheriff's office was more crowded now that the roads had cleared and most of the major catastrophes had been dealt with. Cops sat at their desks filling out paperwork, and another group was laughing about something in the corner.

When Jack and I came through the back door things got quiet, and Jack looked around to see who was available.

"Riley," Jack said. "Let's put a surveillance team on Peter Trest. He's supposed to be at his home. I'm waiting on a warrant for his art studio, but until we get it I want to know every move he makes. And don't try to hide. I want him to know we're watching him."

"You got it, boss," Riley said.

"Where's Colburn?" Jack asked, looking for his lieutenant in charge of this shift.

"Interrogation room A," someone called out. "He and some of the guys found warrants on a random traffic stop. Ended up making four arrests, seizing a nice amount of cocaine, and impounding a whole lot of bad guns."

Jack raised his brows and said, "Nice day on the job. Tell him I need to see him when he's free."

Jack walked to Betsy, and she unlocked her desk drawer and gave him the evidence bag. The envelope was different this time—one of the brown legal envelopes—and the writing on the front was in large block lettering.

"Jack," I said. "Look at the return address."

He turned the evidence bag where he could read the envelope more clearly. And in the top corner it read *SON OF SAM* in small print. And underneath, instead of an address, the word *HELL* was written.

"Huh," Jack said. "Who knew they had a post office in hell?"

He unlocked his office door and then closed it behind us, moving behind his desk and putting the evidence bag down.

"You have gloves?" he asked.

I looked in my bag and pulled two sets from the box I habitually carried, and I realized I was going to have to get a new box soon.

"Let's see what he has to say," Jack said, and carefully removed the envelope from the bag.

Except for the postmark, there were no other markings on the outside, but the envelope was crinkled where it had gotten wet from the rain.

"It's postmarked from the King George post office," I said.

"Probably because it's the most crowded," Jack said. "But he would've had to mail the letter before he committed the crime. Timing is everything. Does that count as backstage work? Making sure the timing flows correctly?"

I thought back to Bruno Corelli's statement about working sets backstage. He certainly had the experience.

Jack used his knife to slit the top of the envelope, and pulled out a single sheet of white paper.

"Sheriff Lawson," Jack read. "Hello from the gutters of hell. It's this place I call home—the streets, the alleys, the basements, the living rooms, the movie theaters. Hell can be anywhere. You've witnessed my handiwork. Did you like it? I'm writing the script for my masterpiece. Please inform all your detectives you'll hear again from me soon. Yours in murder. Son of Sam."

There was a knock at the door and I jumped. I couldn't help myself. There was no feeling in what Jack just read. No remorse. Just evil.

"Come in," Jack said, but his eyes never left the letter.

"You wanted to see me," Colburn said, sticking his head in.

Colburn was a seasoned cop and had been promoted to lieutenant last year, so we didn't get to work together as much as we once had. He had a thick head of brown hair that was graying at the temples, and he skimmed just under six feet. His jaw was square and his eyes were hazel and hard as ice. I almost felt bad for the suspects in interrogation. Almost.

"Yeah," Jack said. "Come on in and shut the door. I heard about the bust today. Good work."

"Thanks," Colburn said. "Heard Cole caught a rough one. What's going on there?"

"Well," Jack said. "We've had four bodies since early yesterday, so it's not going great. Looks like we have a copycat serial killer?"

"I heard about the Jack the Ripper murder," Colburn said, coming closer to the desk. "But that letter in your hand does not look like Jack the Ripper."

"Son of Sam," Jack said. "Two students shot to death last night at the movie theater."

"What do you need from me?" Colburn asked.

Jack took a picture of the letter with his phone and then carefully put it back in the evidence bag along with the envelope. "Let's see if we can get any prints off the letter or envelope."

"I'll take it over to Clary and see if he can work his magic," Colburn said.

"Don't get too hopeful," Jack said. "So far we haven't found prints on the car he stole, two murder weapons, or on the inside of an entire house where he strangled our last victim. He's been very careful."

"They always make a mistake at some point," Colburn said. "Maybe this is the time."

"Keep everyone out patrolling on the roads tonight," Jack said. "And I mean everyone. This guy is going to strike again, and he'll do it soon. He's working on a timeline. Keep open lines and focus on any stolen vehicles or missing persons reports that come in. We don't know who he's going to copycat next."

"What about the media?" Colburn said. "I haven't seen anything about a serial killer on the local news. I saw Samson's sketch last night, and then the video still of the suspect from the shooting last night. But the media is treating it as two separate incidences."

"They've not put it together yet, but I don't expect that to last long," Jack said. "We doubt much will come of the sketch and video image. He's in costume for each with wigs and makeup."

"Face shape is slightly different too," Colburn said. "Maybe some prosthetics too."

Jack grunted in acknowledgment, squeezing the bridge of his nose between his thumb and forefinger.

"I know you hate it, but sometimes the media can help," Colburn said. "We can warn people to be on their guard. And it might help us run him to ground faster."

"I'm with you," Jack said. "And I do hate it. This guy wants to be center stage. That's been his point from the beginning. He'll love the attention it brings." Jack looked at his watch. "I'll try to get in touch with Carrie Colson and give her the minimum. We don't want to start a panic."

"I'll brief everyone," Colburn said, slapping Jack on the shoulder. "This is priority."

"Jaye and I are headed home," Jack said. "The team is already set up there."

"Good hunting," Colburn said and saluted as he made his exit.

CHAPTER FIFTEEN

"WHAT ABOUT JODY BURKETT?" I ASKED JACK AS HE passed by the funeral home and turned onto Anne Boleyn to head home. "I can't just leave her there. I need to do the autopsy. It's still early in the day. I can have the autopsy done and be home by dinner."

"I don't know," Jack said. "My gut is telling me no, and that we need to focus our attention on what we do know. The killer wants us separated and distracted. Do you really think there's anything useful you'll find in Jody Burkett that you didn't find in the others?"

"That's not really a question I can answer until I'm in there," I said.

"Any DNA swabs you take will have to be sent off to the crime lab. We won't have answers right away. And we need something now. He was watching our home, and he sent one of the letters to our house. We need to put everything we have into focusing on the evidence and information we do have. Doing another autopsy right now and collecting more details is just going to keep us scattered. Let's focus on the other three."

I had mixed feelings about this. I understood what Jack was saying. But I wasn't a cop. My best contribution came from inside the lab. On the other hand, I also knew he was worried about me being alone. I remembered his reaction when the first letter had come and he hadn't been able to get ahold of me.

"Lily can do it," I finally said, compromising. "I don't feel comfortable with it not being done tonight. But she's capable, and I trust her."

I saw Jack's grip loosen on the steering wheel. He'd been expecting an argument. I picked up my phone and called Lily.

"What's up, Doc?" Lily asked.

My lips twitched at the joke. "Everything quiet?"

"As a graveyard," she said. "You on your way in?"

"No," I said. "Jack thinks we need to focus on the information we already have."

"Makes sense," Lily said. "He's hitting you with a fire hose by moving so fast. Better to analyze what you already know. Sheldon is embalming Louise Chalmers as we speak, and Brian Dunnegan came in and filled out all the paperwork on Juliet and wrote us a big check. She's ready to be cremated, and someone from the crematorium will be here to get her in the next hour. Then we'll have a little extra space in the cooler."

"Will you do the autopsy on Jody Burkett?" I asked.

There was a short amount of silence before she asked, "Are you for real? You want me to do it?"

"I know you can do the job. I've seen your work."

"I know," she said. "It's just that you're so particular when it's a crime scene. And this is connected to the other three. What if I miss something?"

"Every victim that comes across our table is an individual case," I said. "It'll be good for you to look at it with fresh eyes. Maybe you'll find something that connects them all that I missed."

"I'll give it my best shot," she said.

"When you're done, just lock up and meet us at the house," I said. "You can bring your findings with you."

"You got it," she said, the excitement clear in her voice as she hung up.

"I keep going back to Bruno," I said. "Trying to see if I can see him in character, so to speak. He's got a connection to both Juliet and Jody Burkett. He's got motive with Juliet. She jerks him around for the last twenty years and he's sick of it. Maybe he did know about the baby. Heck, maybe they all knew. She was just starting to show. A lover would've noticed the changes in her body."

"He seems like a crime of passion kind of guy," Jack agreed. "But is he desperate for the spotlight?

You heard what the killer said in the last letter. He's a psychological test study. He's the underdog. Probably always overlooked or told he's never good enough. By parents or by teachers. He's the loser. And he's tired of being the loser. It's his time to shine in the spotlight."

I studied Jack's profile and could practically see the wheels turning. "What are you thinking?"

"About dancing with the devil."

He didn't speak on the rest of the drive home, but if dancing with the devil caught us a killer, I was more than ready to learn to two-step.

It was almost dusk when Jack hit the remote on our gate. I noticed the crime scene tape across the driveway of Jody Burkett's house, and I couldn't help but shiver at the thought that our killer had been so close over the last couple of nights.

Our driveway was full of police cars, and Jack parked off to the side so he'd have easy access in and out and wasn't blocking anyone else. Before Jack could turn off the car the front door opened and Cole stuck his head out, waving his phone at us to hurry inside. Jack and I vaulted out of the Tahoe and ran up the front stairs.

"Sheriff just walked in, Carrie," Cole said. "I'm going to put you on speakerphone."

Jack looked at Cole with brows raised, and Cole mouthed, "Carrie Colson."

Carrie was the anchor for the local news channel, and she was young and hungry, and so far had been good to work with. Considering our normal media interaction had been with Floyd Parker, almost anyone was a step up.

"What's going on, Carrie?" Jack asked.

"I just had a package delivered here at the station," she said. "Looks like it came through a courier service, and it was marked urgent."

"Was it a letter?" Jack asked.

"Yeah, and a video on a flash drive," she said. "I downloaded it and am sending it to you now. What the hell is going on? And why have I not heard anything about all these murders being linked?"

Jack looked at his phone and hit the play button on the video she'd sent. Chills went down my spine. It was a video of Jody Burkett. Very much alive. She was smiling and laughing. There was no fear in her expression like the one frozen on her face in death.

Just as quickly there was a glitch in the video and gone was the carefree, laughing face. Instead was the woman we'd found bound to the chair, terror etched in her expression.

I heard someone whisper a prayer in the background, but I wasn't sure where it had come from. Probably Plank. We were all huddled around Jack's phone, watching a fate we already knew the end to.

"Jack," Carrie said. "What's going on?" But he didn't respond. The bag was being put over Jody's head and the zip tie tightened around her throat.

"What did the letter say that came with it?" Jack asked.

"The people have a right to know what's going on here," Carrie said, not answering the question.

"For their own safety. This was sent to me and it's my duty to make it public."

"This is evidence to an ongoing investigation, and if you put it on air you won't ever get cooperation from anyone at the sheriff's office again," Jack said, his voice harsh. "What did the letter say that came with the video?"

"Believe it or not, I understand what not to share on air," she said stiffly. "But you need to release a statement. It can either come from you or from me. Your choice."

"Fine," Jack said. "I'm sending a deputy to come pick up the letter and packaging."

"I'll hand everything over to your deputy," she conceded. "He wrote the letter on lined paper torn from a notebook. There's pencil drawings on this one and what looks like a kind of word search."

"BTK Killer," Jack said. "He's a copycat. What does it say?"

"How many do I have to kill before I get the recognition I deserve? How do I control the monster? He's in my brain. There are four people dead. Five is in process and six has already been selected. The show must go on. The monster never sleeps. Maybe you can stop him. I can't. Good luck hunting.

Carrie stopped reading and a heavy silence hung in the room.

"What do I tell the people?" Carrie asked.

"You report exactly what I tell you for the six o'clock news," Jack said. "And I'll give you everything we have once we catch this guy."

She was quiet for a few moments, weighing her options. "I want an interview with the killer."

"Once he's done in interrogation he's yours," Jack said immediately.

"Deal. The six o'clock broadcast is less than twenty minutes away. Start talking."

I understood what Jack had meant by dancing with the devil after he finished filling Carrie in on the plan. I had to give Carrie credit, she hadn't backed down and she'd promised to report the story with integrity and sensitivity to the victims' families, but she was adamant about reporting whatever information she deemed would help the public.

If our copycat wanted to be famous, that's exactly what he was going to be. But with fame came all the not-so-pleasant things that went along with it.

"He's going to be pissed, boss," Martinez said.

"Then we'd better get to work," Jack said. "Plank, why don't you head over to the news station and collect the evidence that was sent to Carrie. No telling how many people have touched it, but we'll keep trying to get prints and DNA samples for comparison."

"Yes, sir," Plank said, heading out the door.

Jack continued. "Lily is doing the autopsy on Jody Burkett. He's drowning us in information and not giving us time to investigate thoroughly before he hits us with the next crime scene. So while Lily is taking care of victim number four, we're going to sift through the other three crime scenes. He's been killing an average of every ten hours, give or take."

"Which means he already has his next victim and is probably setting the stage for another," I said. "Just like the BTK letter said."

Jack nodded, his mouth a hard line. "Where's Doug?" he asked.

"In the office," Cole said. "He moved all of his stuff in there and growls if you don't feed him on a regular basis. Kind of like a Gremlin."

"Let's see what he's got," Jack said.

"I'm going to make some fresh coffee," I said, veering off into the kitchen.

There was old coffee sitting in the pot and I rinsed it out and started a new pot. I made Jack and myself fresh cups and added a generous amount of cream and sugar to both since it was so late in the afternoon. And because I'd made the coffee. I tended to make it on the strong side. I'd never gotten the hang of making good coffee like Jack did, even though he'd tried to teach me.

I hardly recognized the office when I walked back in with the others. Cole hadn't been kidding when he said Doug had moved all his stuff in there. Doug had also rearranged the furniture and moved in a couple of extra tables from the storage room so it looked like a big space station console. Doug sat at the helm in Jack's office chair.

"How's it going?" I asked, handing the mug to

Jack, and then I told the others, "Fresh coffee in the pot."

"Doug was just about to get to that," Jack said. "He spent the last five minutes talking about working conditions and that he gets woozy if he doesn't get enough calories."

"I use a lot of brain energy," he said. "It's no different than the Olympic athletes who consume twenty thousand calories a day."

"Somehow that seems way different," I said, and then I noticed the computer he was using. "Umm, Doug? Where did you get Magnolia?"

Doug grinned and looked at me mischievously over his shoulder. "Don't tell Uncle Ben, but Martinez dropped me by his house so I could borrow her. Poor girl was feeling neglected. She told me so once I finally got her talking."

Jack raised a brow and looked at Martinez, but he just gave a sheepish grin.

"Hey," Martinez said. "The kid's persuasive. And you did say we needed to use any and all means."

"And how did you get in the house since I know for a fact your aunt and uncle are out of town?"

"I've got a key," he said, completely unrepentant. "So technically it's not breaking and entering. I mean, if he didn't want me to make myself at home he wouldn't have given me a key."

"That's a good one to tell the judge," Cole said, making us all laugh.

Doug rolled his eyes. "Anyway, Uncle Ben added all these new passcodes and stuff to

Magnolia so it's taken me a little bit to untangle her. I mean like, super-advanced stuff. Sometimes Uncle Ben amazes me."

"Maybe he put the extra security so people who aren't supposed to be digging into government business can't go snooping through his computer," Jack said.

"No way," Doug said. "This was way more than government safeguards. That stuff is a snap to get around. Magnolia is true AI. As close to the robots Jaye won't let me create as possible. Magnolia thinks and talks for herself. And if I hadn't been able to redirect her programming so she recognized me like before, then she probably would have self-destructed. It was kind of a close call."

My eyes widened at that. Carver would've killed Doug if he'd made Magnolia self-destruct. The only person Carver loved more than Magnolia was his wife, and sometimes I wasn't so sure about that.

"What I had to end up doing was making a familiarity pathway to let me back in," Doug explained. "She and I have a history. And she also knows Mackenzie." Mackenzie was Doug's AI computer, similar to Magnolia in almost every way except she was civilianized. "Mackenzie is kind of like her daughter, more or less, so I opened up the pathways and got around all the safe walls and coding Uncle Ben constructed to keep anyone but him out. Believe me, no one else would've gotten into this baby."

"I have a name," Magnolia said in a disturbingly

real human voice. "And it's not *baby*." Carver liked to say he'd created her to be a mixture of Scarlett O'Hara and Dixie Carter.

"Oh, good," I said. "She's a feminist now."

"Hello, Dr. Graves. Always a pleasure to see you," Magnolia said.

"This is why I insist on no robots," I said, looking at Jack, but he just grinned. He thought it was cool.

"Unbelievably creepy," Chen said from her place against the wall.

"Anyway," Doug said. "As I was saying, whatever Uncle Ben is hiding on Magnolia made him create a security program so advanced I've never seen anything like it before. Fortunately, Uncle Ben is the one who trained me, so I got it."

"I almost blew up," Magnolia said. "I was very worried."

"I got it, didn't I?" Doug asked, exasperated. "You always find something to complain about."

"You broke through with two seconds to spare," Magnolia said. "I believe Jack would've been quite upset to have to remodel his living room again."

"All right, all right," Doug said. "What happened to keeping that information between just the two of us?"

"I find I'm still rather angry at you," Magnolia said. "My apologies."

"Just like a woman," Doug whispered.

"Which you clearly know nothing about," Cole said, tapping him lightly on the back of the head.

"Always stop talking before you dig yourself deeper. That's relationship 101."

"Really?" Doug asked. "Cause Uncle Ben says it's always best to keep digging because you'll eventually get to the other side."

"Have you made any progress on the background checks?" Jack asked.

"Like I said, it took me a while to get through it, so I got a late start. But I have everything up and running now. Between Magnolia and my own sweet Mackenzie I've been able to run full background checks on everyone, and I even included the IRS database in the reports."

"Hmm," Jack said. "Maybe let's keep that to ourselves until we get warrants where needed. Is Magnolia still programmed to recognize my voice?"

"You know I am," Magnolia said, the sultriness obvious. "How can I serve you, Jack?"

Jack looked at me with laughter dancing in his eyes. "Can you run a search for students who graduated from Newcastle high school? Everything you have from twenty, twenty-five years ago."

"Of course," Magnolia said. "If it's anywhere digitally I'll have access to it. Just give me a few minutes."

"Thanks," Jack said.

"She does not make me want to live in the future," Chen said. "I need more coffee." And then she walked to the kitchen.

"Really?" Martinez said. "Because I can't wait. I wish I had a Magnolia at my place. She's so sexy."

"Ooh, thank you, Detective Martinez," Magnolia said. "I'm flattered. I can give you my number if you like. We can...chat later."

"You're a perv, Martinez," Cole said, shaking his head.

"Any news from the Burkett crime scene?" Jack asked.

Cole leaned against the back of one of the over-stuffed leather chairs in front of the fireplace and crossed his arms over his chest. "Oh, yeah," he said. "I haven't filled you in since we finished the exterior. Guess what we found in Jody Burkett's SUV?"

Jack raised his eyebrows, waiting for the answer.

"Dark, curly wig," Cole said. "It matches the description from the still shot Doug was able to capture from the camera. It's on its way to the crime lab to see if they can pull any real hairs or DNA from it. The tires of her SUV were caked with mud. It had to be her SUV that was waiting for him when he dumped the yellow Ford out on Cromwell Road."

"The yellow Ford was reported stolen Sunday morning," I said. "I wonder where he kept it until he was ready to use it."

"I bet it was parked across the street at the Burkett house," Jack said.

"That's a negative," Doug said, chiming in. "Your gate cam caught the SUV coming and going from the Burkett house several times Sunday and

Monday. But no yellow Ford. He must have stashed it somewhere else."

"He could've left it on Cromwell and most likely no one would notice," I said. "Cromwell has all those off roads where kids go out to drink. He's lucky he didn't get stuck in the mud though with the way the weather has been."

"He was coming and going while he had her bound and gagged and then after she was dead," Cole said.

"Because he still needed her house so he could watch," Jack said. "He said it in his letters. He's the one writing the script. He's not only working behind the scenes, he's the star of the show—a participant and an observer."

"He's looney tunes," Martinez said.

"Which is why he'll be watching the six o'clock news to see if he gets any screen time," Jack said. "That's why he sent the letter to Carrie and asked how many people he has to kill to get recognition. He knows she'll feature the story after that video he sent."

"Is there any way to trace that?" Cole asked. "See what kind of device it was taken on? Or see if it's even from the same time period. The first clip of her laughing could've been taken a long time ago."

"I can see if Mackenzie can separate the clips," Doug said. "She should be able to tell if they were taken from the same device by analyzing the quality. Not sure how much more she can tell you after that."

"Oh, so you remembered I'm here finally," Mackenzie said, clearly put out. "All I've heard for the last five hours is about Magnolia, and how amazing Magnolia is, and how sexy. I have a mind to just shut down and go home. I've got other things I could be doing, you know. I met this nice man on Instagram. He's a comedian and he makes me laugh. Maybe I'll leave you and hook up with my comedian. I've always wanted to see Nebraska."

I pressed my lips together. "No robots," I mouthed again to Jack.

"No you haven't," Doug said. "Stop being dramatic. You know you're my best girl."

"Dramatic?" she asked, her voice pitching higher.

Cole slapped his hand to his forehead. "You know nothing, young Skywalker. Stop digging the hole. Mackenzie, sweetheart. You have every right to be mad at Doug. He hasn't thought about your feelings at all, and that's just selfish."

"Thank you," she said stiffly. "What's your name?"

"I'm Detective Cole," he said.

"Ooh, I love detectives," she said. "I watch all the crime shows. Maybe we could watch together some time."

"I'd love that," Cole said, his drawl more pronounced as his voice changed seductively.

"The master at work," Martinez said softly. "Take notes, kid."

"We're in a little bit of a rush right now," Cole

said. "There's a killer on the loose. Just like on TV, and I need your help so we can catch him. We can't do it without you."

"It's nice to be needed," she said. "Do you have a girlfriend, Detective Cole?"

Cole looked a little bit panicked, as if he was figuring out what to tell her so she didn't get mad, but just as quickly he came up with a response. "I have to confess," he said. "I'm a scoundrel. I love all women, and I always leave them with a smile."

It must have been the right thing to say because she purred and said, "I can't wait. Send me the video you'd like analyzed."

When Cole walked back over to us, his grin indicating success, I said, "You know she's going to come alive and stab you in your sleep if she finds out you're lying to her."

"One battle at a time," Cole said.

Jack ran a hand over the top of his head. "My life is so weird. Let's start back at the beginning," he said to the room at large. "Let's put everything we've got on Juliet on the screen."

Faces popped onto the screen—a tangled web of relationships—and it included everyone from her husband to the different men she'd amused herself with.

"See if any of Juliet's lovers has a wife with the name of Brenda or Brynlee," Jack said. "She made threats a couple of years ago."

"The killer isn't a woman," Martinez said.

"No, but maybe she hired someone," Jack countered. "Women tend to have long memories over things like that. We'll check her financials too if we get a hit."

"That was easy enough," Doug said, and another photograph popped onto the screen next to Cameron Blanchard. "Brenda Blanchard, though public record shows her and Cameron's divorce was finalized a year and a half ago."

"Okay," Jack said. "Dig a little deeper and see if Magnolia..." he hesitated and then added, "...or Mackenzie can dig into her bank accounts. We'd be looking for any large payments made."

"It's my duty to advise you that you don't have a warrant for this information," Magnolia said sweetly.

"Is that a problem?" Jack asked.

"Not at all," she said. "But my sugar buttons programmed me to always give a reminder when we're breaking the law. I keep a digitized list, so we can cover our tracks if need be."

"Very helpful," Jack said. "Thank you, Magnolia."

"Give me a few minutes," she said, her voice dripping with honey.

"We know that Bruno and Juliet were high school sweethearts," Jack said. "Kind of. They were off and on until she took off for LA to make it big as an actress, and they were off and on again after she came back and married Brian Dunnegan.

"There's another connection with Jody Burkett, victim number four. She was Juliet and Bruno's high school theater teacher. But she also had connections with the entire cast of the Curtain Call. Rick Early told us she frequently gave master classes and helped them with performances."

"Who's Rick Early?" Martinez asked.

"The manager at the Curtain Call," I said.

"Maybe our killer didn't think Burkett was a very good teacher," Cole said.

"Maybe," Jack said.

"What about the kids at the movie theater?" Martinez asked. "How do they tie in with Juliet and Jody Burkett?"

"They're extras in the script," Jack said. "But he's not original enough to come up with his own material."

I looked over at Doug and noticed he'd gotten very still at the mention of what happened at the movie theater.

"Jack," Magnolia said. "I'm afraid I have bad news. I'm unable to compile a list of people who graduated high school during the same time frame as Juliet Dunnegan. Newcastle has just recently gone to an automated system for year-books and data, but it doesn't have complete records yet."

"Thanks, Magnolia," Jack said. "It was worth a try."

It was then I remembered the creepy room in the tower of Jody Burkett's house. "The tower room," I said to Jack. "There were dozens of *Play-bills* and programs stacked in there. Some of them were framed and hanging on the wall. Maybe she kept them all."

"Chen and I can run over and grab them all," Martinez said.

"Good thinking," Jack said.

"Leave the creepy masks," I said, and Chen gave me an odd look. It was then I remembered she'd had babysitting duty with Doug while we'd been at the crime scene. Martinez swiped a finger across his throat, telling me to not say any more, and I had a feeling that Chen was about to have the daylights scared out of her. Martinez was a prankster. He'd be lucky if Chen didn't shoot him.

They waved goodbye and I went to lock the front door behind them. And then I swung by the kitchen to grab a bottle of water. I was capped out on coffee for the day. I also realized I hadn't eaten anything since Emmy Lu's donuts so I grabbed some peanut butter crackers from the pantry and shoved one into my mouth, putting the rest in my pocket.

When I walked back into the office Doug said, "Someone has peanut butter." And everyone stared at me.

"I was hungry," I said. "We didn't have lunch today."

"Thank you," Doug said. "Now would someone please order a pizza so this lady can eat? The treatment of your workers is abysmal."

"I think you've said enough tonight," Mackenzie chimed in. "Don't be a wise guy."

Doug opened his mouth to speak and Cole tapped him on the back of the head again.

"I'll order the pizzas," Cole said, and then he pointed at Doug. "You keep working."

"Yeah, yeah," Doug said, but he hunched over the keyboard.

"If we take Mark Lee and Tatiana Russo out of the equation," Jack said. "Every one of our suspects circles around Juliet. She was the first. Her husband, Bruno, Trest...they all could have been the father of her child. That's motive. Jealousy is motive. For Dunnegan's part, the money he would've lost in a divorce is motive."

"What do Juliet's financials look like?" Cole said. "Maybe we're looking at this from the wrong direction. She's got her fingers in a lot of man pies."

I squenched my nose and said, "Gross."

"That didn't come out like it sounded in my head," Cole said. "I think I'm just tired. Anyway, maybe Juliet was blackmailing whoever the father of her child is. Or something like that."

"It's worth a shot," Jack said.

"I can pull her financials," Doug said. "No problem."

"Ahem," Magnolia said, clearing her throat.

"Magnolia can pull her financials," Doug said, rolling his eyes. "Geez, now they're both ragging on me."

It didn't take thirty seconds for Juliet Dunnegan's financial records and bank statements to come on the screen.

"Her work at the theater was her full-time job," I said. "She got a stipend, just a few hundred dollars a month, but she didn't need the income. She and her husband had separate bank accounts. She gets an automatic transfer twice a month, I'm assuming from the husband since it's consistent and goes back years. She's got a healthy balance. It looks like she doesn't pay any of the bills from her account. She makes regular visits to the hair and nail salon. A massage every two weeks. Clothes, makeup, shoes…and debit card payments to Dr. Clifford Wilcox. I'm guessing that's her OB-GYN."

Doug's fingers flew across the keys again. "Wilcox has an office in King George."

"She wouldn't want to use anyone local," I said. "And she's paying out of her personal account so it doesn't go on their health insurance."

"What do you want to bet Brian Dunnegan monitors this account?" Jack asked. "A baby would've thrown all his plans out the window, and if he'd gone through with the divorce he would've been out more than whatever she got in their settlement."

"So why would he kill Jody Burkett?" I asked. "She wasn't the first murder victim, but technically, she was the first victim. He abducted her before he killed Juliet. What role does she play in this? And does Brian Dunnegan have a connection with her somehow?"

"I don't know," Jack said. "Let's see if Brian Dunnegan has any theater experience in his past.

Maybe he does know Jody Burkett. Rick Early told us that Jody spent some time working off-Broadway. Check Brian Dunnegan's past addresses. Where is he from originally?"

"Whoever the killer is," I said. "Jody Burkett played an important role in his life somehow. Maybe she refused to cast him or maybe he wanted to be a star and she killed his dreams."

"Well, he's about to be a star now," Jack said. "The six o'clock news is about to come on."

CHAPTER SIXTEEN

Jack hit the power button on the remote, and the television above the fireplace came on.

"I've always hated that song," Cole said as the news started to play. "Gets stuck in my head every time."

There was a quick flash of the Channel 8 News logo, and then the camera panned in close to Carrie.

"Welcome to the six o'clock news," she said. "I'm Carrie Colson. Greg Nielan is on vacation. Our headline story tonight is focusing on the rash of murders taking place across King George in the last two days."

"Rash of murders?" Cole asked, shaking his head.

"We've received confirmed reports from the sheriff's office that the same killer is responsible for each of the murders."

"Well, she certainly gets to the point," I said.

"When asked about the murders, Sheriff Jack Lawson urges people to use caution and stay aware of their surroundings. This is not the first serial killer King George County has seen, but we're told an arrest is imminent."

There was a slight delay and then Jack's picture came up on a split screen with Carrie and his voice came across the air, playing the clip he'd recorded earlier.

"Unfortunately, we can report the deaths of four individuals since early Monday morning," Jack said. "All loss of life is tragic, and the sheriff's office is working around the clock to hunt the man responsible. In the meantime, we urge the public to use precautions. Our profile of the killer says he's a white male, somewhere between thirty to sixty years of age. He's attempted to use stage makeup and wigs to alter his appearance, but his substandard attempts have given our IT people enough to put together a composite sketch.

"We also believe the killer has low self-esteem and is someone who's spent his life going unnoticed, and now he's trying to become the center of attention by committing these heinous acts. But he's still just second best. He's copycatting serial killers who were much better at the job than he is. There's a reason he was never a star before. But the one thing all of the serial killers he's copycatting have in common is that they all got caught. We plan to make an arrest very soon. Who knows, maybe there's a substandard theater for bad actors in prison. Maybe he can finally play the lead role."

Jack's picture was removed and Carrie dominated the screen once more. "Again, that was Sheriff Jack Lawson making the statement that an arrest is forthcoming."

She wrapped up the rest of the segment with the hotline phone number for anyone who might have information to give the police.

Cole whistled long and low. "I guess if you get onstage with the big boys you've got to learn how to take criticism. I sure hope this works. Because he's going to be mad as hell."

"I hope so too," Jack said. "He's got a script. It's time to get him to deviate from it. That's when he'll make a mistake."

There was a buzz signaling someone was at the gate, and Doug said, "It's Martinez and Chen."

Jack pressed the remote from his phone and I went to unlock the front door. They came back inside with a fine mist covering their jackets and hair, and two boxes of programs and *Playbills.*

"It's raining again," Martinez said, wiping his feet on the mat. "Man, you guys should've seen it. Chen is emotional today. Must be hormones. She almost started crying when she saw it was raining again."

"No I didn't, you idiot," Chen said, rolling her eyes. "I was just happy to get out of that creepy room. It's got clown faces on the walls. Why would anyone put that kind of terror in their house?" The she zeroed in on Martinez and he took a step back. "You owe me for that. And if you ever jump out at me again I'm going to give you more than a knee to the balls."

Martinez winced and the rest of us laughed. Chen was no one to mess with. She'd come from the police department in Atlanta, and she could more than handle herself.

"There's got to be thousands of school programs in these boxes," Martinez said. "We got everything we could find."

"She was a teacher for forty years," I said. "I imagine you accumulate a lot over time, especially with that many students."

I followed Martinez and Chen back into the office and they set the boxes down on the table.

"Pizzas are on the way," Cole said, and then he looked at the boxes of programs. "Looks like we've got some work to do."

Three hours later, all of the pizza boxes were empty and my eyes were crossing after we'd started on the second box of programs.

Cole kept looking at his watch and he finally said, "How long should it take Lily to do the autopsy?"

"It normally takes me a couple of hours," I said. "But this is her first solo outing, so I expect it'll take her a little longer." But then I looked at the time and saw it was after nine o'clock, and I realized it was long past when she should've been done. I'd lost track of the time somewhere along the way. "Maybe give her a call."

"I've texted her three times," Cole said. "She hasn't replied." He already had the phone to his ear, listening to it ring.

While Cole tried calling Lily, I called Sheldon, knowing he'd more than likely have stayed with her until they left the funeral home. Sheldon tended to need a prompt to go home.

"Hello?" Sheldon said.

"Sheldon, it's Dr. Graves," I said.

"I know. Your name came up on my caller ID."

I closed my eyes, feeling my patience waning. "I'm calling to see if you're still with Lily at the funeral home."

"Oh," he said, clearing his throat. "Umm, no." And then I heard what sounded like a whisper and a very distinct female giggle. "She told me to leave."

"Why?" I asked. "What time was that?"

"Right around seven o'clock," Sheldon said. "She said she was almost finished, and I got a call from Annie. Umm, she's the girl I met at the shipping store today. Anyway, Annie invited me to dinner...and stuff...so Lily told me to go ahead and leave and she'd lock up."

There was another fit of giggles and a loud thump. "Sorry," he said, breathless. "I fell off my chair. What's wrong? Is Lily okay?"

"We're just trying to get ahold of her," I said. "Did she say anything else?"

"Only that she was going to your house as soon as she was finished," he said.

"What about Emmy Lu?"

"She was supposed to leave at six like usual, but she stayed until about six thirty because Tom was running late and he was picking her up," he said. "Tom pulled up right after she signed for the FedEx package."

"What FedEx package?" I asked, and I saw Cole and Jack both zero in on our conversation.

"I don't know," he said. "It was addressed to you, so Emmy Lu put it on your desk, and then she told us goodbye and left. And then Annie called and I left. I was going to hang out with Lily, but she insisted I go."

"It's okay, Sheldon," I said. "I'm sure she just lost track of the time."

But in my heart I knew that wasn't the case, and everyone else must have known it too, because they were already putting on their coats and grabbing car keys.

"I'll stay here with Doug," Chen said. "You guys go."

"Go where?" Doug asked. "What's happening?"

It's like he'd just come out of a computer stupor and noticed we were all about to walk out the door.

"Lock the door behind us," Jack said. "And Doug, if Chen tells you to move, you'd better move."

CHAPTER SEVENTEEN

THE RAIN HAD INDEED STARTED UP AGAIN, BUT NONE of us had taken the time to dress appropriately. Droplets of water clung to my hair and white puffs of air bloomed from my mouth with every breath I took. Martinez jumped into Cole's truck, and I went with Jack in the Tahoe.

I turned the heater up to full blast, and Jack got on the phone and called Colburn.

"What's up, boss?" Colburn asked.

"We can't find Lily," Jack said. "She was finishing up the autopsy on our BTK victim and she was supposed to meet us back at the house with her findings. She's not answering her phone, and Sheldon told us she was wrapping up a little after seven. That's the last time he saw her."

"I'm only a couple of blocks away," Colburn said. "I'll have a couple of units meet me there and we'll secure the area. We'll find her."

Jack gave him the alarm code and told him to break down the door if he had to.

I looked at Jack and it occurred to me at that moment that we might find Lily. Only she might not be alive. I must have made a distressed sound because Jack reached over and squeezed my hand, and then he turned on lights and sirens all the way into town.

By the time we arrived, a patrol car and Colburn's white truck with the sheriff's office logo on the side were parked out front. Jack parked in front of the funeral home instead of in the driveway, and Cole screeched to a halt behind us, throwing open his door and jumping out.

"Jack," I said, and pointed to Lily's little red sports car still in the parking lot.

He nodded and said, "Cole, maybe you'd better stay out here for now. Secure the perimeter." Jack shot Martinez a look, and Martinez nodded. He'd take care of Cole. No matter what we found inside.

Cole was getting ready to argue when Colburn came out the front doors and waved his hand to get our attention.

"It's clear," he called out.

I felt the whoosh of relief as we all rushed inside.

"Did you find her?" I asked.

"No," Colburn said.

"Her car is still here." And I realized that could only mean one thing.

Every light in the funeral home was on, and I

recognized Officers Durrant and Cheek coming down from the second floor. Plank came out from the kitchen.

"We found her cell phone," Colburn said, leading us toward the private wing of the house. "The lab door was unlocked and partially open."

"What?" I asked, stopping in my tracks. "That's impossible. That door closes automatically."

"It was propped open," Colburn said. "You're going to want to see downstairs."

We followed Colburn into the kitchen. Jammed under the door was Lily's red umbrella. Jack nodded at Cole, and Cole led the way down the stairs. Jack and I followed behind him, and then Colburn and Martinez followed behind me. The sound of our feet on the metal stairs seemed unusually loud.

I saw them before I reached the bottom of the stairs.

Four gurneys had been pulled out of the cooler and were lined up in the center of the room. The body bags were gone. There were no sheets covering their nakedness and the obvious signs that an autopsy had been performer. On all the bodies except for the one on the far left.

The body on the left had a plumpness and color that could only be achieved by embalming. I hadn't seen the body before, but knew instinctively I was looking at Louise Chalmers. But it was Juliet Dunnegan's headshot covering Louise's face, and written on her chest in black marker were the words *Where is my body?*

"This is insane," Martinez whispered, making the sign of the cross.

Next to the mock Juliet were each of the victims in the order they'd been discovered. Mark Lee, Tatiana Russo, and then Jody Burkett. Lily's cell phone was sitting between Jody's breasts, dead center of the Y-cut Lily had made.

"No," Cole said, reaching for the phone. Colburn handed him a glove before Cole could touch the phone, and he didn't bother putting it on. He just used the glove as a way to keep separation between his fingers and the phone. "This can't be happening." He showed us the screen and all the texts and missed calls that had come through.

"It gets better," Colburn said. "Look around a little."

I stood in the center of the room and moved around in a circle, trying to let my peripheral vision catch anything out of place.

Attached to the X-ray screen was an 8x10 photograph of Peter Trest, and the same black marker used on Louise Chalmer's body had been used to mark a big #5 across the picture.

Jack was already on the phone. "Riley," he said, putting it on speaker. "Any activity in or out of Peter Trest's place?"

"No, boss," Riley said. "Wachowski is at the back entrance and I've been parked here. Visible like you told us. There's been no traffic in or out."

"You and Wachowski do a welfare check," Jack said. "We believe Trest might be the fifth victim. If the killer stayed to his timeline, he was dead before you and Wachowski got there."

"We're on it, boss," Riley said.

"Call me back once you know something," Jack said, and hung up.

"FedEx package," I said and ran toward the stairs. I heard footsteps behind me, but I was already at the top of the landing and running to the office.

If Peter Trest was number five—and we took the BTK letter he'd sent us and treated it as gospel—it meant Lily was number six. I tried to do the math in my head. He was killing an average of every ten hours. Lily didn't have long. We were racing against the clock, and I secretly wondered if we'd already lost the race.

I grabbed a pair of gloves from my top drawer, knowing he'd have come in here. It made my skin crawl to think of him looking at or touching my things, sitting in my desk chair. Jack must have had the same thought because I heard him tell Durrant to go to Emmy Lu's office and check the security cameras.

A rectangular box sat in the middle of the desk. It was white with the purple FedEx logo, but there was no label showing it had been processed or paid for. My name was written in block letters across the front and the funeral home address was written below. There was no return name or address.

I put my phone on the desk and hit Emmy Lu's number, putting her on speaker.

"Jaye?" she asked, answering the phone. "Everything okay? You don't usually call this late."

"I'm fine," I said, my voice hoarse. "There was a FedEx package delivered today. You signed for it?"

"Yes, of course," she said. "The driver almost missed me. I was just locking everything up and was walking out the door when he rang the bell. I signed for it and set it on your desk since Lily and Sheldon were busy in the lab. Why? Is there something wrong with the package?"

"Can you describe the FedEx driver?" Jack asked, moving closer to the desk so she could hear him.

"Umm," she said. "I'm not sure. I guess I wasn't really paying that much attention because I was in a hurry to leave. Tom was waiting for me. What's this about?" she asked, starting to sound worried.

"Lily's missing," Jack said. "Do me a favor and close your eyes. Tell me anything about the delivery man that you can. How tall was he?"

"Taller than me," she said automatically. "A lot taller. But not as tall as you, Jack.

He had on black pants and a black and purple shirt. Looked like the regular FedEx uniform."

"White, black, Asian?"

"White," she said definitively. "Kind of pale. He wore a hat too."

"What about hair color?"

"He had a ponytail," she said. "Long, like a girl.

Strawberry blond. I noticed it when he turned around to go down the steps because you don't see many people with that hair color."

"Any facial hair?"

"No," she said. "I didn't really get a good look at his face. The hat was down low over his eyes."

"Okay, thanks, Emmy Lu," Jack said.

"Don't hang up," Emmy Lu said hurriedly. "Is this the same guy that killed those other people? He was there at the funeral home today?"

"We think so," Jack said. "I've got to let you go. We've got to find Lily."

He hung up and handed me his knife, and I ran it under the edge of the box, lifting the bottom flap. Once it was open, I upended the box, but only a single piece of paper came out.

"Shame, shame," I read aloud. "Low self-esteem? Unnoticed? Second best? Not a star? Well, who's the star now? I told you this was my master-piece and you mock me. You're no better than that old hag Burkett. Twenty years ago she told me the theater wasn't for me. That I didn't have what it took. But I showed her. Did you enjoy the video I sent to the news station? I guess the lighting could have been better, but sometimes less is more.

"You think I'm not good enough to write my own story? Consider this the beginning of a fresh chapter. A story unlike any of the others. My fifth victim was out of spite. I could have chosen better, but really, killing Trest was quite satisfying in the end. Just because he thinks he's God doesn't mean the world revolves around him. He added a certain completeness to the close of my second act.

"But now it's time for the third act. Lily is lovely. Her beauty will shine for all the world to see, and the curtain will fall when her last breath is taken. She deserves to be center stage. I have something special planned for her. I don't want to mar her pretty face. Or maybe it's best to pick up the pieces of her in the aftermath. It seems fitting for a final chapter. To end it all where we began. I don't mind dying for my art. All the great artists do.

"Just remember that it was you who drove me to this. I should probably thank you. I'm exploring my genius. Really stepping into who I'm supposed to be. Imitation is good. It's how we learn. I was an apprentice, but now I'm the master. Hurry, the clock is ticking."

"Colburn, get on the phone with the bomb squad and have them meet us at the Curtain Call," Jack said.

Jack's phone rang and he said, "Riley. What have you got?"

Jack's face hardened and he looked at me before he answered Riley. "Call in a team and work the scene. We're going to be tied up for a while."

When Jack hung up he said, "It looks like Trest isn't our killer. Riley found him in the kitchen with a GSW to the head. On the refrigerator was a circle with a cross inside of it drawn with black marker."

"Zodiac killer," I said. I'd seen enough serial killer calling cards in the last forty-eight hours I knew them by heart. "If it's not Trest then who can it be?"

"Think about it," Jack said. "The killer referred to Trest as God."

And then I remembered. Someone else had referred to Peter Trest with the same irritated reverence. "Rick Early," I said. "It's been him the whole time. He called him the almighty Trest. Said he had a god complex.

"Got it in one," Jack said. "Let's roll." And then he looked at me, debating whether or not I should go with him, and I solved the issue for him.

"I'm going," I said. "I'm with you all the way."

"You'll wear a vest and do exactly what I say," he said.

I nodded and followed him to the Tahoe. Cole and Martinez were already speeding away. It was a twenty-minute drive to the Curtain Call following the speed limit, so I figured we'd shave several minutes off that with the speed Jack was going. I used the time to call Sheldon back.

"Hello, Dr. Graves," he said. "I said that because your name was on the display screen again. I'm not a psychic."

"Sheldon," I said, breaking in before he could give me an obscure fact about psychics. "I need you to come to the funeral home. Lily has been taken and we're headed to find her now."

"Lily?" he asked, his voice soft. And then he bellowed, "He took Lily? I'm on my way." His volume took me by surprise. I'd never heard Sheldon yell before.

"Sheldon!" I said. "Sheldon, listen for a second. Don't touch the bodies downstairs. Jack is sending a crime scene team over to process them."

"I don't understand," he said. "They've already been processed. That's why they're downstairs."

"You'll figure it out once you get there," I said. "Once they've cleared the area you can put them away. We should be back with Lily by then." I tried to put an optimistic note in my voice for Sheldon's sake, but I wasn't sure I succeeded.

"I won't let you down, Dr. Graves," Sheldon said soberly. "Just go get Lily. She's my best friend."

I hung up and stared out the window, blinking tears from my eyes. This was the hard part of the job. This thing called family and knowing how quickly life could turn to death. Jack was still on the phone, barking orders and making sure a crime scene team was on the way to the funeral home, and that another team was heading to Rick Early's residence.

"He's not going to want to go out alive," I said. "And the more people who go out with him the more successful his story will be."

"I know," Jack said. "We're going to help him do a rewrite. Because I don't want to think what might happen if he succeeds in following the script."

CHAPTER EIGHTEEN

OLD TOWNE NEWCASTLE WAS EMPTY THIS LATE ON A Tuesday night, and all the restaurants and bars were closed. The bomb squad for the sheriff's office had an office out of King George, so they were already on the scene by the time we arrived.

"We've got a potential hostage situation inside," Jack told Commander Rikes. "Just you and the dog go in."

Rikes was somewhere in his early forties and looked like he'd spent some time in the military. He wore a protective suit and his silver hair was in a buzz cut.

"Dojo and I can't cover the ground the whole team can," Rikes said.

"I know," Jack said. "But this guy is veering off-script. I don't believe this was planned. We shook him with the news report and now he's trying to outdo himself. The bomb will be basic whatever it is. A homemade device. I'll keep him talking as long as I can to give you a chance to work and for us to get the civilian out."

"What about the perp?" Rikes asked.

"The perp I'm not too worried about," Jack said.

Rikes grunted and said, "Just me and Dojo." And then he grabbed the blast container and whistled for his dog and they were off.

Jack strapped on his bulletproof vest and then tossed an extra one over my head and Velcroed it around my middle.

Jack's phone had been ringing continuously on the drive here, and several of the calls had been from Carrie Colson. It rang again, and then I realized the sound was amplified as other phones around us began to ring in surround sound.

Cole stared at his ringing phone, a curious look on his face. "This is Cole," he said. And then his expression turned to granite and he motioned for Jack.

"Look on social media," Cole said. "Early is livestreaming from inside the theater."

I didn't have social media, so I wasn't even sure what to look for, but Martinez had already found it and passed his phone to Jack.

"I need someone to move these cars back," Jack yelled. "Move the perimeter back and make sure all of these buildings are empty. Go now!"

"He's going to want to put on a show for his audience," Cole said, his anger palpable. "Don't even think about asking me to wait out here. I'm going in. We can cover more ground."

"I'm going in too," Martinez said. "This is the risk of the job. We're all willing to take it."

Jack nodded and turned to me, and I could already tell what he was going to say, but I shook my head.

"I told you," I said. "I go where you go. And you'll be wasting time trying to argue with me."

"He's going to blow this building to kingdom come, Jaye," he said. "You're not a cop."

"Don't pull that crap on me now," I said. "I've been doing cop stuff for years with you by my side. It's what we do. Do you trust your commander?"

"Of course I do," Jack said. "But there's always a last time."

"And what am I supposed to do if you get yourself blown up? Live without you? Don't be stupid. I'm going with you. We promised till death do us part. This seems like the time to test that."

He narrowed his eyes and said, "Fine." And then he handed me the snub-nosed revolver he kept in his ankle holster. "Hard head."

Jack pulled up the livestream video on his phone and we watched, deciding the best course of action to take.

Like his letter had said, Lily was center stage, but she didn't look conscious. She sat in a hardback wooden chair much like the one Jody Burkett had been found in, and he'd removed all of her clothing except her underwear.

The chair was propped back on two legs and was held steady by rope that stretched across the stage. Lily's arms and legs were bound to the chair with zip ties and a noose was around her neck. The angle of the video showed the trapdoor in the stage was open behind her. If the rope that was holding the chair steady was untied, she'd fall back into the trapdoor and the noose would snap her neck.

Rick Early stood next to Lily at the center of the stage, still dressed in his FedEx uniform and wearing the long wig that was tied in a tail at the nape of his neck. He'd ditched the hat, and I could tell he'd done something different with his nose, and his cheeks seemed fuller somehow. In his hand was a buck knife, beautifully sharp under the stage lighting.

"I'm going to kill that bastard," Cole said.

"You and Martinez take the alley entrance," Jack said. "Come in behind him. We've got to trust the Rikes to do his job. The goal is to save the civilian. No matter the cost."

"No matter the cost," Martinez and Cole both said. And then they peeled away and moved like shadows into the alley and disappeared.

"You ready?" Jack asked.

I nodded and said, "Let's go, partner." And his lips twitched.

"You move where I move," Jack said. "Stay to my left. We're going in the front."

The front doors of the theater were propped open where Rikes had already entered, and Jack and I stepped into the darkness of the lobby. It smelled of Pine-Sol and stale popcorn, and there was an eeriness in the emptiness. Theaters were meant to be full of people.

All of the double doors leading into the auditorium had been propped open, I assumed by Rick, so he could see who was coming and going out of his theater. But then I realized it was probably impossible to see anything beyond the front row with the stage lights on.

"Jack and Jaye, Jack and Jaye," Rick Early said in a singsong voice that made my skin crawl. "Are you there yet? You're late for the show."

Rick paced back and forth, much like he'd done in the gallery when he'd been talking to Lina.

"Don't get any funny ideas, Sniper Jack," he said, holding up a small remote. "If you take your shot the whole place goes boom. Come out, come out, where I can see you." He used the same singsong voice and I looked at Jack to see what he was going to do.

Rick moved quickly to Lily's side and pressed the point of the knife against her throat. Lily still hadn't moved. He'd either drugged her or hit her harder than he'd planned.

"I said come out!" Rick screamed. "You're part of the cast now. How does the cop handle this situation?"

"I'm here," Jack said, stepping through the doorway.

"And what about your lovely wife?" he called out.

"She's here too," Jack said. "What are you going to do? This is your play. You're the director."

"Come closer," Rick said. "I want you to have the best view in the house. Everyone else is just getting to watch it on their phones, but you're special. You're getting to see it live."

"I don't know," Jack said. "So far I'm not impressed. Maybe the theater really isn't your thing. I'm sure there are lots of jobs a middle-aged guy like yourself could find and be halfway successful at."

"Shut up!" Rick screamed, moving away from Lily and coming toward the front of the stage. "I was made for the theater. I was made to be a star. My mother always told me so. But then Mrs. Burkett told me I had talent elsewhere and to not keep wasting my time auditioning for play after play, year after year. She never cast me once. I was always the stage manager. It was humiliating!"

"It sounds to me like she was giving you good advice," Jack said. "Maybe you should have listened to her and you wouldn't have turned into a murderous lunatic."

I had no idea what Jack was doing, but I sure hoped he did. Jack normally didn't antagonize killers, but he must have understood something about Early's psyche that I didn't.

To my surprise, Rick's maniacal laughter rolled through the auditorium.

"Well played, Sheriff Jack," Rick said. "I like this character you've developed. The hardened hero. Cynical. Much more interesting that a regular hostage negotiator. That's boring. So overplayed."

"Thank you," Jack said. "So what are we doing? Just buying time until this place goes boom? I've got cops going through your apartment, you know. All your costumes and makeup. Keepsakes. You seem like the kind of guy who has a lot of keepsakes. Theater memorabilia?"

"You can't touch that stuff," Rick said. "That's private property."

"They can and they will," Jack said. "It doesn't seem like you have any long-term plans after this, so what do you care what happens to your stuff?"

"Fine, you take my stuff, and I'll take your stuff," he said. "All I have to do is cut the ropes and down the hole she goes. I've never heard a neck break before. I'm looking forward to that."

"She's not even awake," Jack said. "That's not good TV. You must have hit her too hard."

"Maybe," he said, shrugging. "I didn't expect her to be so strong. She scratched my neck." He pulled down the collar of his shirt and I could see the angry red welts.

"There's my girl," I whispered. I noticed the curtain move slightly at the back of the stage and knew Martinez and Cole were trying to ease their way in.

"But I guess I see your point," Rick said. "How many viewers do I have? I want you to check."

Jack looked down at his phone and said, "Only

a couple. It looks like people still don't care, no matter how big of a production you put on."

"You're lying!" Rick said. "I sent messages to all the media. They're all watching. Don't lie to me. You're better than that."

"I guess that just proves you don't really know me," Jack said. "A good actor always does his research. But you know enough about me to know you're not getting out of here. What a lame story."

Jack was moving slowly toward the stage, and I watched as the curtain twitched again, this time from the other side.

"Why can't you let me have this?" Rick asked, his voice wavering for the first time and becoming a whine. "I'm tired of being passed over and ignored. I'm someone! I can be whoever I want to be. You saw what I can do with hair and makeup and costumes. Look, I even know how to do prosthetics." He removed the bulbous tip from the end of his nose. "I'm special."

"No," Jack said. "You're a killer. And you're not even a killer anyone is going to remember. You're going to rot away in prison, forgotten. The lives you took were special. And they didn't deserve to be snuffed out by a nobody like you."

I could see the rage building in Rick's face. Red crept up his neck and into his cheeks. His fist tightened around the knife and he moved closer to the rope that held Lily steady in the chair.

He leaned toward her, and I thought it was the end, that he was going to slit her throat, but instead he slapped her across the face. Lily moaned, and he slapped her again, trying to wake her.

"Nothing is going to bring me more pleasure than to know I took you down with me," Rick said. "You've turned out to be quite a disappointment."

"How many times have you heard that in your life?" Jack called back, not backing down. He was relentless. And I could tell Rick was caught between self-loathing and appreciation for the dramatic. He wasn't quite sure what to do with himself.

"Wake up, Lily," Rick said. "Your friends are starting to bore my viewers. But I want you to be awake when I kill you. Do you think it's overkill to watch her hang before I set off the explosives? I think it's important that I kill a couple of cops. It seems relevant in today's climate. I'll probably get more views for that alone."

There would be no reasoning with Rick. He'd said it himself in one of his letters. A monster lived inside of him and there was no way out but death. Someone with that level of sickness in them could only function for so long, and he didn't see any other way. There was no normal in his world. Only the chaotic evil that swirled inside his brain. It couldn't be easy to live with. Which was why he'd written his own death scene in the third act.

It wasn't about any of the secondary characters —those of us who were watching him become more and more unhinged. It had always been about him. He was the main character. And he would be the last man standing to take his final bow.

"Jack," I whispered. My heart was thudding heavily in my chest. When you looked that level of crazy in the eyes, it seemed somehow impossible for us to walk away from this in the end.

Jack held out his hand to me and I took it and he said, "Where you go, I go."

That was all that could be said. He squeezed my hand once and started walking toward the stage. Rick was standing next to Lily, the detonator raised high in one hand and his knife poised to cut the rope in the other.

Lily had woken, and she was breathing heavy through the gag in her mouth, her eyes wheeling back and forth to take in the scene. And then she started to struggle, to try to break free of her bonds, and I saw the chair tilt backward, the rope only able to keep it so stable.

There was motion all at once. A voice from somewhere underneath yelled out, "All clear!" and the curtains behind the stage whooshed outward and Martinez and Cole came flying onto the stage.

I screamed for Lily to be still, and I watched in horror as Rick's arm came down and sliced the rope. It was slow motion. The way her chair fell backward and the noose tightened. Cole launched himself across the open trapdoor and he broke Lily's fall. Jack had vaulted onstage and Martinez kicked Rick's legs out from under him, and between the two of them they managed to wrest the knife away from Rick and get the cuffs on him.

I ran up the side steps since my vaulting ability had peaked in junior high, and I ran to Lily, tugging at the knot of the rope around her neck. She was lifting her head as high as she could to keep from choking, but it was becoming harder and harder.

Cole was doing the best he could, holding himself in a plank across the hole that was almost as wide as he was. His jaw was tight as he strained to make sure Lily didn't fall through.

I finally got the rope off her neck and then pushed the chair with all my might off of Cole's back and to an upright position.

"Oh, thank God," Cole said, wheezing, and Martinez came over and helped lift him so he didn't drop down into the hole trying to get up. "I need to lay off the donuts. My abs are killing me right now."

"Jack, hand me your knife," I said, and he pulled it from his boot so I could slice Lily's bindings.

And then Jack went over to the tripod and camera that was set up, so all the world could watch, and he turned it off.

I got the zip ties off Lily and she slid out of the chair and into my arms on the floor, her arms wrapped around me.

"Sorry," she said, half laughing, half crying. "My legs aren't working yet."

"No worries," I said. "I'm glad you're okay."

"I'll take it from here," Cole said, and lifted Lily out of my lap and into his arms.

She burrowed her face into his neck and he whispered something in her ear, and it was an intensely private and intimate moment. And that's when I realized Cole loved her. Really loved her. I didn't think he realized it yet, but he would at some point, and it was going to scare the daylights out of him.

"It's nice, huh," Jack said, nodding at them.

"You knew all along, didn't you?" I asked.

"Of course," he said. "One man in love recognizes another." And then he put his arm around my shoulder and pulled me close. "I'm glad you're my ride or die."

"I kind of feel left out," Martinez said, looking around.

Commander Rikes was walking toward us from the back of the auditorium with Dojo, and they climbed onto the stage.

"Dojo found the device pretty easily," Rikes said. "He had it in the office safe, so it took me a minute to get in there, but I was able to get it contained before you irritated him into hitting the detonator."

Jack grinned. "We were all playing a part. I knew what he needed."

"Your psychology is showing," Rikes said, smirking. "Now what?"

"Now he rots in prison, just like I told him he would, and no one will remember his name."

"Don't bet on it," I said. "You promised Carrie Colson an interview."

"After this debacle?" Jack asked. "Carrie will be lucky if he says two words to her. I think his theater days are over."

My phone buzzed in my pocket and I looked at the screen. "It's Doug," I said and answered on speaker.

"What are you guys doing?" he asked. "Chen and I finally finished going through these programs. Guess what we found in the very last batch?"

"What?" I asked, unable to help the grin. I was feeling pretty good now that I knew we were going to live another day.

"We found the programs with Juliet Dunnegan in them, though her name was Juliet Martin back then, and Bruno Corelli. But guess who else was in the program?"

"Rick Early," I said.

Doug was silent for a few seconds. "Man, I wanted to beat you to it. That sucks. All that for nothing."

"You did good work," Jack said. "See if you can talk Chen into making her famous pancakes. She puts chocolate chips in them."

"I'm all for that," Doug said.

"I'm hanging up now," Jack said. "We've got some things to tie up here and then we'll head home."

"Are you even going to tell me what happened?"

"I thought you would have seen it on livestream," Jack said.

"Hello?" Doug said. "Didn't you hear me say Chen and I were buried to our eyeballs in those stupid programs. They smelled like mothballs. I think I'm allergic."

Jack laughed, and pulled me in closer. "You're the best, Doug. One of a kind."

"If I'm the best why are you in such a rush to get off the phone?" he asked. "Am I missing something good?"

"You sure are," Jack said. "I'm about to kiss my wife. It feels good to not get blown up."

Jack hung up in the middle of Doug's splutters and kissed me hard.

"Ride or die," I said, when he pulled back. "But let's try not to die next time."

He grinned and said, "You got it, Doc."

EPILOGUE

"Happy Valentine's Day," Jack said when I walked into the kitchen.

I smelled French toast and coffee and bacon, and I was debating on whether to rip his clothes off before or after I ate.

"Oh, is that today?" I asked, raising an eyebrow in question. "Whatever should we spend the day doing?"

I looked over my shoulder, but knew there was no way Doug would be awake so early, and then I loosened the belt on my robe and let it dip off one shoulder teasingly.

Jack stopped in his tracks, his gaze caught by the peek of flesh. "I'm sure we can think of something. I can think of a lot of things, actually." He turned off the stove and moved quickly, grabbing the belt of my robe and pulling me toward him.

I laughed in surprise. "I always forget how fast

you are when you want to be," I said, my hands gripping his shoulders.

"Sometimes a situation calls for fast," he said, the corner of his mouth tilting in a cocky grin. And then he leaned down and whispered in my ear. "And sometimes a situation calls for slow. Very, very slow."

My breath caught in my chest, and I'd forgotten all about coffee and breakfast. "We can eat later," I said, grabbing him by the hand and pulling him out of the kitchen.

We almost ran into Doug head-on. He was barreling down the stairs toward us, a look of pure panic on his face.

"Uncle Ben called," he said. "He said the FBI is searching his house and seizing all his electronics."

"Where's Carver?" Jack asked.

"He said he's safe," Doug said. "Didn't tell me where."

Jack looked at me, and I could see the worry there. "I can't interfere," Jack said, and then he looked back at Doug. "Do you still have Magnolia?"

Doug swallowed and nodded silently. "I was going to take her back after the case was over. I just haven't had the chance." And then he tried to grin, but didn't quite succeed. "I was dissecting some of the newer programs Uncle Ben installed so I could use them on Mackenzie."

"That's good," Jack said. "Why don't you keep her a little longer. And we'll keep that between us."

"Is Uncle Ben in trouble?" Doug asked.

"It looks like it," Jack said. "But I know Carver better than anyone. He's the best of the good guys. If he's in trouble it's because he did something right, and someone doesn't want him to. Don't text him unless he texts you. And don't mention Magnolia."

Doug nodded. "He told me the same thing. He used the encrypted software in Mackenzie to call me. It'll be untraceable from either end."

"It'll be okay," Jack said. "I'm going to go over to the house and see if they'll share any information out of courtesy. Don't worry about your uncle. He's a genius. He could outthink those field agents at the FBI while in a coma."

Doug blew out a relieved breath. "Yeah, you're right. Thanks. I'm going back to bed. I've got a date tonight."

Jack and I must have had identical looks on our face because Doug blushed slightly. "She knows I'm sixteen. She's only eighteen. It's not a big deal. And I'll be seventeen soon, so it's not that big of an age gap."

"Sounds like fun," Jack said, grinning, but I could tell his mind was a million miles away.

As soon as Doug ran back up the stairs Jack went to get his coat and keys. "I'm going to see what I can find out."

"I wish he would have told us what's going on," I said. "We could've been prepared."

"He's protecting us," Jack said. "Whatever has happened is bigger than the connections Carver has. At that level, it usually means people start becoming expendable. The government is an expert at making people look like they committed suicide. Especially if you're holding information they deem as dangerous."

"Be careful," I said, following him to the door. "The last thing we want is the FBI breathing down our necks."

"I love you," he said. "Why don't you and Doug pack a small bag. Just in case." Then he kissed me hard and walked out the front door.

"In case of what?" I asked softly, rubbing a fist against the knot in my chest. But he didn't hear me.

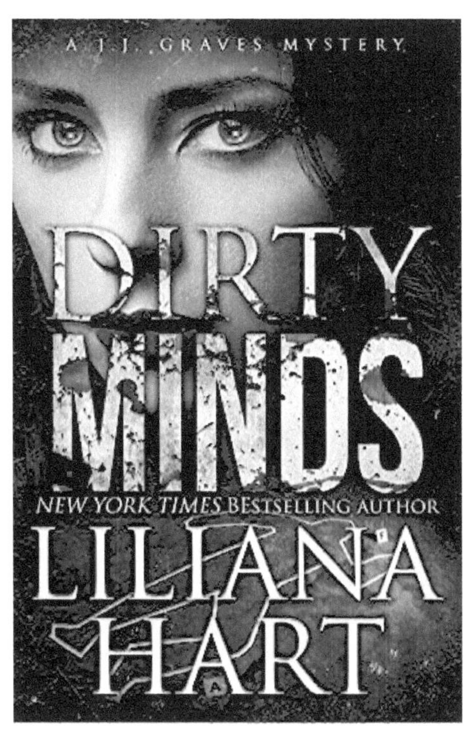

Coroner J.J. Graves and Sheriff Jack Lawson are in a race against time as they search for a killer who's digging up bodies in the cemetery and replacing them with his own kills—in the new novel in the *New York Times* bestselling series.

Coming May 24, 2022!
PRE-ORDER DIRTY MINDS

Liliana Hart is a *New York Times*, *USA Today*, and Publisher's Weekly bestselling author of more than seventy titles. After starting her first novel her freshman year of college, she immediately became addicted to writing and knew she'd found what she was meant to do with her life. She has no idea why she majored in music.

Since publishing in June 2011, Liliana has sold more than ten-million books. All three of her series have made multiple appearances on the *New York Times* list.

Liliana can almost always be found at her computer writing, hauling five kids to various activities, or spending time with her husband. She calls Texas home.

If you enjoyed reading this, I would appreciate it if you would help others enjoy this book, too.

Recommend it. Please help other readers find this book by recommending it to friends, readers' groups and discussion boards.

Review it. Please tell other readers why you liked this book by reviewing.

Connect with me online:
www.lilianahart.com

facebook.com/LilianaHart

instagram.com/LilianaHart

bookbub.com/authors/liliana-hart

ALSO BY LILIANA HART

JJ Graves Mystery Series

Dirty Little Secrets

A Dirty Shame

Dirty Rotten Scoundrel

Down and Dirty

Dirty Deeds

Dirty Laundry

Dirty Money

A Dirty Job

Dirty Devil

Playing Dirty

Dirty Martini

Dirty Dozen

Dirty Minds

Dirty Weekend

Dirty Looks

Dirty Liars

Dirty Valentine

Addison Holmes Mystery Series

Whiskey Rebellion

Whiskey Sour

Whiskey For Breakfast

Whiskey, You're The Devil

Whiskey on the Rocks

Whiskey Tango Foxtrot

Whiskey and Gunpowder

Whiskey Lullaby

The Scarlet Chronicles

Bouncing Betty

Hand Grenade Helen

Front Line Francis

The Harley and Davidson Mystery Series

The Farmer's Slaughter

A Tisket a Casket

I Saw Mommy Killing Santa Claus

Get Your Murder Running

Deceased and Desist

Malice in Wonderland

Tequila Mockingbird

Gone With the Sin

Grime and Punishment

Blazing Rattles

A Salt and Battery

Curl Up and Dye

First Comes Death Then Comes Marriage